KU-766-284

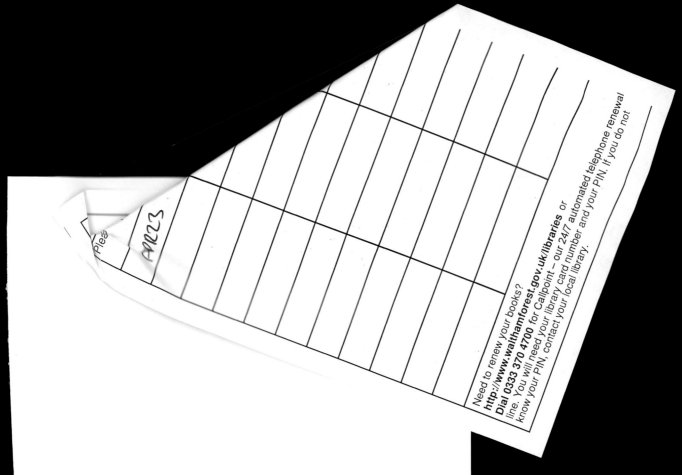

Need to renew your books?

http://www.walthamforest.gov.uk/libraries or
Dial 0333 370 4700 for Callpoint – our 24/7 automated telephone renewal
line. You will need your library card number and your PIN. If you do not
know your PIN, contact your local library.

Pleas

M223

WALTHAM FOREST LIBRARIES

904 000 00750648

MAGGIE BLUE
and
THE WHITE CROW

**GUPPY
BOOKS**

ALSO BY ANNA GOODALL

Maggie Blue and the Dark World

MAGGIE BLUE
and
THE WHITE CROW

ANNA GOODALL

**GUPPY
BOOKS**

MAGGIE BLUE AND THE WHITE CROW
is a GUPPY BOOK

First published in the UK in 2023 by
Guppy Books,
Bracken Hill,
Cotswold Road,
Oxford OX2 9JG

Text © Anna Goodall
Illustrations © Sandra Dieckmann

978 1 913101 817

1 3 5 7 9 10 8 6 4 2

The rights of Anna Goodall to be identified as the author of this work has been
asserted in accordance with the Copyright, Designs and Patents Act 1988.

All rights reserved. No part of this publication may be reproduced,
stored in a retrieval system, or transmitted in any form or by
any means, electronic, mechanical, photocopying, recording or
otherwise, without the prior permissions of the publishers.

Papers used by Guppy Books are from well-managed
forests and other responsible sources.

MIX
Paper | Supporting
responsible forestry
FSC® C171272
FSC
www.fsc.org

GUPPY PUBLISHING LTD Reg. No. 11565833

A CIP catalogue record for this book is available from the British Library.

Typeset by Falcon Oast Graphic Art Ltd
Printed and bound in Great Britain by CPI Books Ltd

For Juno

WALTHAM FOREST LIBRARIES	
904 000 00750648	
Askews & Holts	21-Apr-2023
JF STO	C

PART ONE

1

MISTRESS NOBODY

The blue wren was poised on a branch, so light she swayed with it in the breeze that tried and failed to pierce the late June heat. She was watching the girl, as she had watched her through the winter, spring, and now the summer.

Maggie Blue was lying on a rug in the sunshine beside the considerable spread of the one-eyed tabby cat, her trusty companion. The girl was small and slight – she did not take up much room. Her fine hair trailed messily out behind her. Her grey eyes, now closed, were considerably too large for her face and often changed to green or light grey: the colour of the sea in this world.

The wren had not tried to read her; those were not her orders. She had only observed. The girl was shy and there was some deep melancholy in her that Bathsheba couldn't help but feel radiating from her diminutive form. This was alleviated by occasional bursts of laughter, at other times, a fierce anger that lit up her eyes and coloured her skin deep red.

Maggie Blue could cross between the worlds; in this way Bathsheba knew that she was extraordinary. But she spent her life doing very ordinary things. She walked to school; she sat in class; she walked home; she lay on the dusty couch talking to the cat (Bathsheba had never come across a human capable of talking to an animal, that too was curious) and watched images flicker across a paper-thin screen. The girl slept, she bathed remarkably often, she cried occasionally, she had bad dreams, and recently she'd been spending all her time with two other children: one pale and very fair, the other slender and dark.

The sound of a shrill bell rippled out into the garden from an open window of the flat. The girl stirred drowsily then shot up and ran into the house. At the same time every week the metallic rings would summon Maggie to speak into a curious black machine that Ulrich had explained to her was called a telephone.

Bathsheba flitted over to a lilac bush that grew up against the kitchen window so she could peer in and watch the girl standing in the narrow dark hallway. As always when she talked on it at this particular time, a crease appeared in her forehead and her huge eyes seemed to focus on something far away, something that caused her pain.

The wren watched for a little while until she heard a familiar screech coming from the back of the unkempt

4

garden behind her – it meant her grouchy comrade, Ulrich, was ready to take over.

She sang out her trilling melodic response and then, with one more quick glance at Maggie, flitted noiselessly across the garden until she landed upon the great oak. It astonished her, perhaps more than anything else about the people in this world, that they considered trees almost as inanimate objects, as dumb and lifeless as the crumbling brick wall the tree grew beside, on which the fox cubs played at dusk.

She alighted next to the great grey owl and shifted. So that when Ulrich swivelled his enormous head, he saw beside him a very small blue-haired woman with sharp matching blue eyes that were already laughing at him. With anyone else he would have been insulted, but for some reason he couldn't get angry with her.

'What's Mistress Nobody up to today then?' he asked grumpily.

'Not a thing,' Bathsheba replied airily, knowing this would annoy him. 'She's on the telephone.'

'With a night of inactivity to follow, I can only imagine.' Ulrich spat down onto the parched soil below, or spat as well as an owl could, which was not very well at all. 'The day Mistress Nobody does something interesting, believe me, I will go into shock. I think Roda is trying to punish me.' He ruffled the feathers on his great head. 'But for what?'

Without waiting for a reply, he flew up into the air. Bathsheba watched as he landed amidst the leaves of the neighbour's dying ash tree. With his extraordinary sight, he could spy on Maggie from anywhere in the garden. He looked so fierce sitting there, his huge eyes permanently astonished, that Bathsheba began to laugh. If something didn't happen soon he would explode.

But then a sense of bad things to come shivered through her. She stopped laughing – war was raging in her homeland. Soon she would be called away and they would long for these dull boring days on the watch; soon everything would change, and not for the better.

2

THE DINOSAURS

'Did you know that the dinosaurs lived on earth for 165 million years before they became extinct?'

It was the middle of July and boiling hot. In the distance she could hear the shouts of kids playing football and dogs barking and running after balls over the yellowed grass of the big field. The sky was a blue dome above Maggie's head, both endless and bound by some invisible force. Everything was slow and lazy.

Except for Will who kept talking: 'And *we've* only been here for seven million. I mean, isn't that incredible?'

Ida was leaning back on her elbows, the long blades of grass vying to brush against her smooth brown arms. 'Yes, Will, incredible. But it's not like they did anything interesting in their 165 million years, did they? They just ate each other.'

'Well, that's not strictly true. Many of them were herbivores, like the stegosaurus, for example. But anyway, the meteorite is probably the most interesting part,' Will hurried on, trying to hold their attention. 'Everything right at the epicentre was incinerated instantly. Whoosh! The excess carbon in the air destroyed what was left, or almost everything that was left. It was like a nuclear bomb times a million.'

'That's a scientific figure, is it?' Ida asked.

Will continued as if he hadn't noticed the heavy sarcasm. 'Then there was all this dust, so much dust swirling around the entire earth. Seventy-five per cent of all life forms were destroyed. It was dark all the time, no daylight.'

Maggie started slightly and looked over at Ida, but she didn't flinch – she never flinched.

'I mean, actually, we could do our whole project just on the meteorite,' Will said.

Ida sat up now, mockery flickering in her eyes. She smiled. 'I mean we *could*. But then again, who wants to do a project about a lump of rock that took out some reptiles millions of years ago? Come on, Will. It's like medieval people or something. Who cares?'

'And the suffragettes are *so* fascinating?'

'They were brave and brilliant women who changed our world. They paved the way for the opportunities girls and women have today.'

Ida's opinions often sounded like things she'd read in a book that she just parroted out verbatim. The thought flickered into Maggie's mind in unwanted rebellion and she quickly snuffed it out.

Will sniffed. 'I find them boring.'

'Just because they're women.'

'Incorrect.' Will pushed his heavy blond fringe out of his eyes and away from his perspiring forehead, and the thick hair stayed stuck out at a strange angle. Even in the shade it was boiling.

Ida suddenly turned to her. 'What do you think, Maggie?'

Maggie didn't like it when they put the spotlight on her. She blushed slightly and shrugged. 'I'm fine with either.'

Ida and Will both groaned and then carried on arguing. Maggie couldn't understand why they liked to argue with each other so much. For her part, she didn't care whether they did their summer project on dinosaurs, suffragettes, medieval people or medieval people's suffragette dinosaurs. It was all just school to her . . . a monotonous flow of boring tasks and judgements that she never seemed to come out of very well.

Her mind drifted away from their conversation again. She could no longer imagine rain or cold or grey skies; it was like there had always been a heat wave. And she, Ida and Will had always been friends.

At first Ida had used the summer project as the reason to call, but then she'd stopped bothering to explain and Maggie began to assume they would see each other every day. Will and Ida both moaned about how bored they were, so Maggie made sure she did the same. But secretly it was the best summer holiday she'd had for a long time.

After everything that had happened in the Dark World, life had been very calm and very normal. And although when they'd gone back to school in January, Ida hadn't *exactly* kept her promise about them sitting together and everything, she, Helena and Daisy no longer bothered her, and occasionally Ida said hello and smiled. Then Mrs Thomas had put them on the same biology project, and by chance, Will had joined them having come in late from a dentist's appointment. Though Maggie wondered if Mrs Thomas was trying to help her out, because she was bottom of the class, and the other two were at the top.

Will Snowden was kind of a loner, but he had this amazing confidence that seemed to radiate off his helmet of white-blond hair. No one bullied him even though he was a bit of a know-it-all, and he genuinely didn't seem to care what other people thought of him. Maggie wished she could be like that.

After the project, they started doing their homework together in the library occasionally, or Will and Ida did their homework and Maggie copied their answers. Ida even walked home with her once in a while. On these walks Ida never asked Maggie any questions. She just talked about herself and her friends and what they were doing in non-stop chatter. She was careful never to mention the Dark

World or how afraid she'd been or any of the things she'd told Maggie that day in Moss Hill on Christmas Eve. And Maggie understood – she did not want to talk about it either.

And then in the summer holidays they'd formed this unlikely trio. (Helena and Daisy were both away, but still.) Maggie had never been in a group before and it was such a good feeling, the feeling that you belonged with other people. She wasn't going to let anything jeopardise it.

She tugged absentmindedly at the narrow silken end of the French plait Ida had done for her that morning – Ida had pulled her hair so tight it still hurt her scalp. They had looked in the mirror admiring her handiwork and Ida told her she looked amazing, but Maggie knew it was a lie. Especially standing next to Ida. Her hair all scraped back like this only made her huge grey eyes look even bigger and weirder. She would never be beautiful like her friend.

And despite having turned thirteen a few weeks ago, Maggie had barely grown at all. Ida, on the other hand, had got at least two inches taller. This gave Ida's mother the perfect opportunity to give Maggie her daughter's old clothes. Now Maggie had good jeans (albeit with the ends rolled up several times), and lots of expensive T-shirts and jumpers, all still carrying a delicious whiff of the fabric softener the Beechwoods' housekeeper used.

Maggie knew it was very kind, but secretly she couldn't

11

help feeling a solid nugget of shame whenever she thought about it . . . so she tried not to think about it.

The other two were standing up now. Shielding her eyes against the insistent sun, she saw Ida look down at her, a silhouette against the sky. 'Come on.'

Maggie put her old shoes on and the worn inner soles were deliciously cool on her bare feet. Her feet were much smaller than Ida's, which was something of a relief. Her trainers were badly scuffed and had holes in them, but she preferred it to more hand-me-downs – this way she wasn't a total charity case.

They crossed the grass and went up a cool alley between two brick houses until they emerged into a street with a row of shops and an Italian restaurant near to where Will lived. Maggie glanced at Ida and wondered if she'd ever been to Will's house. She thought about Ida's diary: the revelation that Ida actually liked Will, *liked* him. She'd never asked Ida about it, though she kept meaning to. She wondered if they ever spent time together without her? But again, she pushed the thought away. Why was she always trying to ruin things?

They went into the newsagent. It was dark and slightly dank inside. Mr Floros greeted them in his soft high voice with the usual refrain.

'Don't steal anything,' he said from behind his paper.

Will peered into the freezer, trying to make the decision between a Cornetto, a Feast and a Twister. It was a genuinely tough call.

'Are you going anywhere on holiday, Maggie?' he asked, his back still turned to her as he rummaged around in the freezer cabinet. Will was going to Norway to see family and then Spain, and Ida was going to Italy for several weeks.

'Um, we're going back to Norfolk for a bit. Not as exciting as you guys, but . . .' She felt her cheeks redden and inwardly cursed herself for it.

She had no idea why she'd started lying now and again, but little fibs just kept slipping out. Maggie could feel Ida's laughing eyes upon her – her friend had the uncanny ability to know when she was making stuff up – but Maggie didn't turn to meet her gaze. She felt relieved that she didn't feel Ida's emotions any more, or anyone's for that matter. That had all stopped since she had come back from the Dark World.

'Oh, cool. Norfolk's great,' said Will, and he made a grab for a strawberry Cornetto.

When Maggie got back to Milton Lodge, the one being whose mind she could always read was waiting for her on the front door mat. He scowled as she approached and his tail flickered with irritation.

'Is it too much to ask that you or the old bag keep some kind of regular hours? A cat could easily atrophy waiting for one of you to turn up.'

Maggie smiled indulgently as Hoagy, the old one-eyed cat and her best friend, deigned to leave his spot to come and curl around her legs. His soft heavy tail tickled her legs and she stroked his tatty fur as he purred heavily. In truth, Hoagy was not only her best friend; he was the person, or creature, she felt most comfortable with.

They walked together round the side of the house to the messy garden that was yellow and parched, sizzling in the heat. The man on the radio this morning had said it was officially a drought.

Maggie looked up at the heavy blue sky. 'When was the last time it rained, Hoagy?' she asked.

'Pah! How would I know?' he retorted. 'Now are you going to get me the rest of my tuna out of the fridge, or aren't you?'

She opened the back door and found the place empty and full of stale heat. Her Aunt Esme was out, as per usual. 'Come on then.'

It was a source of great frustration and some humiliation to Hoagy that, even teetering on his sturdy hind legs, he wasn't able to open the heavy fridge door. Once Maggie found him, wild with desperation, clawing at the rubber seal trying to get at some scraps of leftover salmon Esme had promised him and then promptly forgotten all about.

Maggie emptied the half tin of tuna into his bowl with a handful of cat kibbles and soon his chops were delicately partaking. Afterwards he came and stretched out on the sofa beside her and began his rigorous cleaning procedure, which took up most of his time, though he always looked exactly the same afterwards.

He had fully recovered from his ordeal in the Dark World, save for the long impressionistic scar that Miss-Cane-the-wolf had ripped down his belly. But the old cat had lost his taste for a fight since only just surviving their adventures. These days he much preferred to be endlessly fussed over and gloriously well fed by Esme, who adored him beyond all reason.

The official line was that since his great adventures in another world, he had become bored by petty suburban squabbles, which were quite frankly beneath him. Thus he had willingly conceded his three-street territory (the evening slot) to a huge slob of a ginger tom called Franz. According to Hoagy, Franz had a violent temper, an intimidating body-weight ratio and an alarmingly fast right hook. He was also two years old. From the comfort of Esme's old sofa cushions, Hoagy assured Maggie that his former streets would not be changing paws for some time. Not that he cared, of course.

Now his one eye looked at her expectantly. Since his recovery, Hoagy's formerly rather esoteric film tastes had relaxed, and he was currently obsessed with comedy films from the eighties and nineties.

'So are we going to watch *Big* or *Mermaids*?'

When Maggie had been recovering from her own injuries inflicted on her by the now-deceased Miss-Cane-the-wolf,

Esme had dug out a TV, an ancient VCR player and some videotapes for them to watch. It turned out she had a surprisingly big and varied collection. These days Maggie and the cat would often sit and watch stuff together, as Hoagy rarely felt like sneaking into the old cinema down the road like he used to.

Esme would join them in the evening sometimes, though of course Maggie's aunt assumed that Hoagy was dozing and/or thinking of chicken, not compiling mental notes on actors and story structure. The videos were often very bad quality and lines would flicker up the screen, or a crucial scene would have been accidentally taped over by a short clip from the *Antiques Roadshow*. But Maggie found their little film club comforting, especially in summer when the warm air wafted in through the open door, and the light from the tiny TV screen illuminated their three faces. It felt like they were a family then, albeit a somewhat unconventional one.

But that afternoon Hoagy really did doze off and after a while, ripples of interference invaded the video just as Tom Hanks was playing 'Chopsticks' on the huge toy-store keyboard. Maggie tried bashing the old TV, but a sea of white-noise snow had descended and eighties New York was lost in the blizzard.

Reluctantly she gave up and turned it off. It was cool in the dusty living room but outside the heat still beat down relentlessly. She felt anxiety gnawing at her: she didn't like to be on her own any more. When there was no one else about, she often thought about the Dark World and what she'd seen there.

In her dreams she would see Mr Yates' awful, distorted face pressed against the hot glass, or Miss Cane-the-wolf coming towards her, or Frank's body lying in the woods, or she would feel Eldrow's hands around her throat. And now she found herself thinking about Dorothea Dot, the old lady, the moon witch and Esme's great friend. She had disappeared suddenly after Christmas . . . apparently without trace, though now they knew . . .

The phone rang in the hall, relieving Maggie of her unwanted thoughts. There was only one phone now – the museum piece that used to sit by the sofa had finally packed up and not been replaced. Maggie made no move to pick up and soon Esme's embarrassing answerphone message played out.

After the beep, a familiar ice-cold voice cut through the hot air: 'Good afternoon, Ms Durand. This is Dr Naradnam calling from the hospital. Please do return my call at your earliest convenience.' Then the line went dead.

Maggie hated this woman's voice. She didn't think anyone with a voice like that could possibly look after or care about anyone else. She always imagined that this doctor considered her mum like some sort of lab rat. She started walking round the living room, unable to be still all of a sudden.

'Could you *please* stop your incessant pacing?' came a grouchy voice from the sofa after a while.

'Could you *please* shut up?' Maggie snapped back.

She didn't bother to wait for Hoagy's response, but burst out into the back garden. The heat rammed into her, but its intensity made her feel better. The old wall at the bottom was still broken down; the garden was still a mess. It pleased her. She walked down and sat on the crumbling pinkish bricks and felt her skin prickling in the sun.

This was the other thing she tried not to think about: her mum. She was still in hospital with severe depression. But Dr Naradnam had phoned one day to say that Cynthia was becoming increasingly paranoid, which was not in line with her usual behaviour. She claimed that someone she knew had been murdered and was convinced that she was being watched and would be next. They had increased her medication, because that was all the doctor ever suggested they do – she didn't seem to have any other advice except 'increase the medication'. Why did it take seven years to learn that?

Esme didn't bother to let Lionel Brown know. Maggie's dad had been in Toronto for the last nine months with his new girlfriend, and had only managed a few postcards and the odd call. Maggie couldn't say she missed him that much and he certainly wouldn't be any help to her mum: he obviously didn't care about either of them at all.

Maggie could feel her nose beginning to burn so she

got up and walked back inside. She needed to pull herself together and stop thinking about the past. The truth was that, in so many ways, her life had never been better. She had friends and a sort-of family. And best of all, she was free. Nothing had happened since her dramatic escape with Ida and Hoagy; the Dark World had let her go for ever.

3

STILL HERE

The man sat motionless in the large oak at the bottom of Maggie's garden, looking fixedly at one spot in the near-distance – the ground floor flat of Milton Lodge. He was huge with great gnarled hands that gripped the thick branch beneath him. He looked exhausted but his eyes were large and staring, and in the dusk they looked bright yellow.

There was a rustling in the bone-dry leaves behind him and Ulrich's great head swivelled round. He was hoping to see Bathsheba, his companion in arms for this tedious task. But no, it was only a squirrel that eyed him with alarm, its tail twitching manically, before rushing off, chittering out a warning.

The man sighed heavily. You were taught never to become fond of your fellow warrior shifters, but he had to admit he had a soft spot for the tiny blue wren. She had been gone far too long and he missed her. He turned back to the lights glowing behind the curtains of Milton Lodge. As per usual, not a thing was happening.

He was a warrior, from a line of warrior shifters, and he was not meant to sit around in trees hour after hour. But all he did was watch over a girl who spent her days hanging about with two other equally useless children and talking to an old cat. It was humiliating. For a moment it seemed that the great hands would snap the bough clean in two. But then the knuckles lost their white tension. Roda the heron, the great warrior shifter, had ordered him to watch the girl. He had no choice but to obey.

The girl could cross between worlds, this much he knew. As far as was known, only shifters could do this. And she could converse with at least one animal . . . that, too, was a shifter trait. But she was also not a shifter; she only had one form. Thus she was a puzzle, but an intensely boring one, as far as Ulrich was concerned.

He sighed with irritation as his huge eyes focused upon a large purple-black shape coming towards him. Duma the giant crow landed heavily on a nearby branch. He was a shifter Ulrich had little time for. He was clumsy and had little warrior spirit despite his size and magnificent glossy feathers.

'Where is Bathsheba?' Ulrich grumbled.

The crow preened himself. 'She has still not returned.'

Ulrich did not like this news, but he communicated nothing of his fear. 'And what of the battles?'

'Sun City has fallen,' Duma reported, as if it wasn't all that much.

The giant man was astonished.

'Roda says the City of Flowers will be next.'

'It's so easy?' Ulrich enquired, equally surprised and concerned there would be nothing left for him to do if and when he finally got back to the Island.

'The moon witches are surprisingly ferocious,' Duma said. 'And the Islanders have little defence now that the seven families have gone'

Ulrich only grunted in response. The entire point of his, of any warrior shifter's existence was to protect the Great O. For many generations that had meant little more than policing the boundaries of her Magic Mountain kingdom and trying to thwart the constant use of the fragile portals by Islanders and lowlier shifters. But now, what was happening felt like it could be a fight for existence itself. And here he was, doing exactly nothing. Really, what was the point?

He brought his knees up to his chest and hugged them, then pressed his thighs in as hard as he could. His body morphed and compressed as he shifted. And now a great grey owl was perched there in the man's place with its look of malignant surprise, the dying red of the sunlight tinting its magnificent feathers. He gruffly instructed Duma to watch the Lodge for the night then he shut his hunter's eyes and went to sleep.

4

THE TERRIBLE ONES

It was a scene of desolation. The huge walls of Sun City were broken and horribly charred, fires still burnt on the ground and Bathsheba could see dried blood smeared on the cobbled streets. The umon shantytown that had once grown like a fungus up the city's side was nothing more than a pile of ash.

Bathsheba circled round again and again, struggling to take in what she was seeing. And then she spotted the survivors: the formerly privileged citizens huddled together in the golden stone square on the far side of the city, mothers comforting their children, elders covered in blankets. Lanterns flickered around them illuminating their frightened faces. They were guarded by umons and small dark figures in black clothing – the victorious moon witches.

The attack on the city had been quick and brutal, and war had now spread across the Island. The moon witches along with rebel umons were attacking the other six cities, and they were all expected to fall soon.

Roda had heard rumours that the Fathers were allowing the moon witches to win the war, that they were abandoning their cities and building a new stronghold in the Magic Mountains. But no warrior shifter had ever seen it. And this was Bathsheba's mission: to find out if the so-called City of Gold really existed.

After taking in the nightmarish ruins of Sun City, Bathsheba flew across the wide fields of dark wheat stretching beyond it to the west. Lanterns were still strung across, but the umons no longer worked there; the crops were diseased and dying. Soon there would be no food. And terrible floods in the north meant that Moon City had almost vanished entirely.

She had heard, too, that the portals were starting to disintegrate. There were stories of those crossing being spat out in the wrong place, a few or many miles from their destination, or in rare cases, never being seen again.

For the first time, Bathsheba felt truly afraid. Things had been bad for a long time, but no one had heeded the warnings and now everything was falling apart. Whoever won or lost the war, it would make no difference. But if the Great O did not come back, the world could no longer survive and, quite simply, there would be nothing left to fight for . . . But it was not her place to give up hope. She must stick to her mission and not think.

The white-time was fading as she flew swiftly over the great lakes and then the pink steppes that glittered exquisitely as dusk fell. She climbed up and over gusts of steam from the hot pools and swooped over the caldera, where the mouth of the volcano had collapsed many moons before. Then, at last, her wings aching, she started the final ascent.

Despite her feelings of dread and despair, nothing could dampen the joy she felt when she finally saw the Magic Mountains once again. The moon shone magnificently ahead of her above the purplish-grey peaks. She climbed a little further in the freezing air until she saw, far below, the verdant fields, forests and lakes of her home.

Now she had reached her destination, Bathsheba felt a profound exhaustion. She descended steeply into the valley and crash-landed in one of the trees, only just managing to hang on to a branch and steady herself. She huddled her tiny beak into her electric-blue feathers and slept.

When she woke she saw the whole glorious plain stretched out before her. It was the most beautiful place. It was lighter here, the plants were still green, and there were a few dark-brown stingbirds that could not survive anywhere else on the Island. She could even see insects moving in the undergrowth – not everything was gone, not yet.

She flew low over the treetops, staying close to the valley's edge in the shadows cast by the mountains rising to the east. The valley was vast and it took Bathsheba some time to cross it. Below her she saw that new paths had been cut through the forest heading to the northern side.

She dropped into the trees just as a phalanx of masked guards appeared, herding umons before them. After they passed, she flitted north-east for some time, until she reached the edge of the trees, and then she saw, rearing up in front of her, a bizarre glittering structure. It shone like madness in the clear light and she had to squint to even look at it.

This area had been the site of dense ancient forest where many of the wisest trees had grown and flourished; now all that was gone as if it had never been. She prayed to the moons that they hadn't destroyed the sacred pool as well.

And was this golden monstrosity supposed to keep the Great O out? Were they building a fortress against her? The little wren shook with righteous anger – the stupidity of it! The Great O was the air they breathed, the water they drank. Bathsheba had given her life in service to the Great O and she swore now that she would never stop fighting this malignant and ridiculous tribe whose only wish seemed to be to tear the world apart. Her heart trembled with anger and some fear, but she went on.

From what she could make out, it was a U-shaped building enclosing a large courtyard. It was almost impossible to look at directly, though she could just make out umons working on the eastern side. It was monstrously magnificent, brutal and stupid at the same time. But it was hardly the citadel Roda had warned her about, the place where the chosen would live whilst others perished. It barely looked big enough for the seven families, let alone the servants, the guards, the supplies . . .

She looked for a way in. On the unfinished side of the building, Bathsheba noticed small windows along the upper storey that as yet had no barriers to prevent unexpected visitors. She waited until there was a lull in the endless movement of guards and worker umons beneath her, then sped out into open ground and headed straight for the windows. As she flew, her feathers twitched sensing other shifters in the vicinity.

Bathsheba got herself tucked into the shadows before she looked down. Almost immediately five orbs swept into the large courtyard below. She knew them at once, but what were they doing here? And then she saw a man she recognised. He was led by masked guards, his hands tied behind his back, his head down. He was tall and stooped, and his body was now thin to the point of frailty. When he glanced up briefly at the golden building, his huge grey eyes were suffused with some strange suffering.

'Eldrow,' she whispered. The former ruler of Sun City had fallen far. And the orbs clearly no longer obeyed him. Was he a prisoner? But why? The guards pushed him roughly through two huge golden doors and the orbs followed behind. A tiny dark-haired boy, flanked by two young women dressed neatly in black, went next. And then came Almarra, the sorcerer. When she too had disappeared from view, the golden doors slammed shut.

Bathsheba flew into the building itself. In marked contrast to the shimmering outer shell, she found herself in a long corridor panelled with the regular black wood of the forests. A little way ahead, small peat lanterns flickered at regular intervals. There was no one to be seen, just the dull noise of hammers behind her as the umons worked on. Of course, there were those who would be able to sense her. But she hoped that the flutter of her tiny heartbeat would barely register in this enormous place.

She flew down the dim corridor and came to a wide stairwell constructed of golden stone with a gold bannister unravelling down and down. And as she peered into the stairwell she got a lurch of intense vertigo: so that was it! The structure went deep underground; the golden corona was just the tip of the iceberg. They were building a bunker, a cave of gigantic proportions where they could hide out during the wars and environmental disasters that now seemed almost inevitable. No wonder they were letting their cities go to the moon witches with almost no resistance. They had abandoned the people to their fate.

On the floor below she saw Eldrow being held by the guards in front of doors emblazoned with suns and strange creatures Bathsheba did not recognise. Slowly the doors opened and Eldrow, the orbs, the tiny boy with the servants and Almarra passed through them. Bathsheba hesitated for a moment: she was here to explore, to find out all she could about the place, but Eldrow's presence was surely significant, something Roda should know about.

The doors were already easing shut so she gave up her cover and flew, at full speed, just over the top of them. She made for the highest point she could, which turned out to be a shallow dome. She found a small promontory at its base where she could perch, and only then did she dare look down.

In a semi-circle beneath, seven figures sat in enormous golden thrones around the sacred pool and to her deep relief she saw that the ancient evergreen tree still grew out of its deep waters. The pool was not meant to be covered: it was supposed to be in the open air, in alignment with the stars that were reflected on its mysterious surface. But they had not destroyed it; that was something.

The figures' faces were hidden within cloaks spun from thread of deepest blue, their gnarled hands were laden with golden rings, and in the water of the pool around which they sat, something dark was lurking. Bathsheba's heart began to speed once again. She strained to see . . . they looked like large snakes with slimy black bodies. They barely moved, but occasionally one would twitch and the surface of the water rippled. And after a moment, Bathsheba began to hear a low and ominous humming in the air that seeped into her head. She knew she had found the Terrible Ones.

Roda had spoken of them once. They had risen up out of the pool when the Great O had vanished. He told her that they could never be ended, and that they ripped their enemies apart with no mercy. The little wren shivered.

Below her the guards pushed Eldrow and Almarra to the floor and one of the hooded figures rose. He spoke in a deep flat voice that resounded around the space. 'Eldrow, because you are of the seven great families, you are being given a chance.'

Bathsheba's attention was drawn to the tiny boy standing just behind Eldrow. His head was bent as if ashamed or penitent. And she could feel, amidst the confusion of signals in the room, his abject terror.

The robed figure continued. 'We know of the ancient moon witch's vision and though we do not set store by pagan rituals, these are strange times. The ancient saw the girl's connection to the Great O. We believe that if she is strong enough to return here, the Great O will seek to destroy us. The girl may help her return and we can take no risks; too much depends upon it.'

Bathsheba was listening intently: so this was why they had spent moons watching the girl – the Great O needed her. Ulrich would be glad to know how important it was after all. But something in her could not believe it. Maggie Blue was so slight and she seemed lost most of the time. All she really wanted was to be normal, pretty, all the banal human things. Bathsheba smiled at the thought. She had become strangely fond of her. Yes, she was odd, certainly, she had something, some power, but the idea that such a slender, clueless girl could affect the fate of this world seemed almost too far-fetched.

There was a long pause during which Eldrow's face dropped closer to the ground in his enactment of grovelling penance, though Bathsheba could sense that it was not at all sincere. Beside him, Almarra's spindly form was trembling – she was truly afraid.

Then the cold detached voice continued, 'You kept the girl's presence hidden from us. You betrayed us and put us all at risk. For this, you have lost your place here. And you will remain outside permanently with the fools and vagabonds unless you can rectify your mistake.'

Eldrow's head was still bowed and his voice at least sounded respectful, even if his thoughts still bubbled with resentment and anger. 'Can my boy stay?'

'No. He goes with you. Your line will perish if you do not complete this task. Bring the girl from the other world to us. The orbs will be returned to you for this, but their loyalty remains here with us. Bring her to us; that is all.'

Bathsheba's eyes had grown wide, or as wide as a tiny wren's eyes could; Roda must be told of all that had passed here. She looked around for an escape route. The shallow dome, decorated with constellations in beaten gold against stone painted a pale celestial blue, was solid, she could see no tiny gaps through which she might squeeze. She could not risk getting trapped here. She would have to try and fly out unseen as the others left through the great doors. It had been risky enough the first time. She sat motionless, waiting for Eldrow and his party to be taken out by the guards.

But Bathsheba, distracted by what she had seen and heard, had let her mind wander from the greatest danger and now she sensed it far too late – a black presence that, despite its size, had left the bottomless pool and was rising swiftly and silently up the wall towards her. The low humming suddenly grew unbearably loud inside her skull.

The great doors were just beginning to open and she wanted to fly but she found that she couldn't move. Instead some invisible force seared its way into her. Before she even had time to gasp, she felt the awful sharp teeth in her mind, ripping at every layer savagely. She wondered if she could shift into her human form to distract it; become the tiny woman with the bright blue hair. But it was far too late. She saw the powerful jaws open, bearing the multitude of small sharp teeth, and the mad-looking white eyes that glowed and glared at her. She cried out in intense pain, her tiny wren's heartbeat trying to fight against the darkness that overwhelmed it, but it was no good.

Her inner life was crushed at the very same instant that the powerful, hinged jaws cracked her small body in two. After a few moments resting on the ledge finishing its morsel, the creature slithered back down the wall, along the stone floor to its masters, back into the dark water that shimmered with reflected gold.

5

A BOY CALLED OZ

A dark-haired boy sat amongst the trees in the great forest by the lake. He was wet and cold, but he had no desire to move. This tree was his favourite. He loved the way its sprawling branches spread so low to the ground, but that it was also one of the tallest in the forest. Its huge, gnarled trunk split off into three magnificent pathways and Oz had chosen the middle route that day. Near the top, the upper branches were strong enough that he could hoist himself up and look out far across the landscape.

It was misty now, but on clear days you could see for miles. To the west were the Magic Mountains from where they had so recently been banished. To the south, the City of Folk, Almarra's old stronghold, where smoke and flames could regularly be seen rising.

A shifter loyal to Almarra – a white mountain cat with purple eyes called Cano – visited them occasionally and reported that the fighting was especially fierce in Folk.

There were more men of fighting age, and the population had been less dependent on *glitra* – the joyfulness powder that everyone had once taken, but which was now completely unobtainable. Cano told them that the very last supplies had been bought using exorbitant amounts of gold by the Fathers as they fled to the Mountains. He also told them that the moon witches were using powerful herbal infusions to poison their enemies as they lay injured on the ground, and that they died in great pain. Oz shivered at the cruelty. The world had changed very quickly.

Looking the other way, to the north-east, he saw the endless black crop plains beyond which lay his home, Sun City, impossible to see because of its position down in the valley. The fighting was over there and the fires had burnt out long ago . . . He had not seen Suri, his beloved nurse, since he'd been taken just before the moon witches had attacked the city. Only occasionally did he allow himself to wonder if she had survived.

The mist was getting denser and he was shivering, so he climbed down a few levels and got comfortable. He often lay in these branches listening to the trees whispering. The ancient bark against his skin was like peace, his body connected to the endless movement and life happening deep within it. Now he watched as freezing ice-rain suddenly began to pierce through the leaves and fall past him, smashing up against the trunk and branches, and wedging into the dark soil beneath. The ice storms were getting more frequent.

Slowly, slowly as the storm eased, the temperature rose again. Now the only sound was of water dripping from the leaves, the cracking of ice and the hum of the trees talking to each other, their indecipherable messages flowing back and forth in a staccato rhythm. But then from somewhere on the forest floor came a yelp of pain.

Oz was immediately on the alert. He shimmied down lower, but could not see anything. The agonised cry came again. He manoeuvred himself to the very lowest branches and hung from his legs to get a better look. The hours he'd spent in these trees, coupled with his small light body, had quickly turned him into a formidable climber.

Beneath him he saw a small umon, a female he guessed, collapsed against a tree trunk nearby. Deep red, almost purplish blood was seeping from a large gash in her side. Oz dropped quietly onto the ground and tiptoed towards the injured creature.

It wasn't rare to see umons fleeing, using their brilliant navigational skills to get away from the fighting. Oz felt sorry for them – their faces were gentle, and they were often badly hurt. Cano had said that the moon witches ended any umon caught trying to escape battle. Were they cowards to run? Oz wasn't sure, but he certainly sympathised.

He had always wanted to be brave, but he was small for his age, and back home the other boys had always teased him. It was well known that he was afraid of Bertan, the tutor, who liked to mete out punishments with his special stick made from an other-world wood called ash. And he was currently afraid of many things: his father, Almarra, the orbs, moon witches, and, more than anything, the dark beings with terrifying white eyes he had glimpsed slithering in the deep pool in the City of Gold.

Oz came up beside the panting umon. 'Can I help?' he whispered.

The umon's head flipped round, immediately on the alert, but it took her some time to focus on him. 'Who are you?' she said eventually.

'I'm no one,' Oz replied. 'Would you like some water?' She drank gratefully from his small umon-skin bottle. He was relieved she didn't notice. 'You've been fighting?' he asked.

She nodded. 'Yes.'

Oz watched as she took out some loose dark leaves from her small sack, crushed them up and pressed them to the worst part of her wound. Perhaps the moon witches gave their own soldiers healing poultices? The umon gasped and her eyes rolled back in her head, but gradually the herbs seemed to soothe her.

Oz knew the umons had a secret network of tunnels that ran all over the Island. Once or twice he had followed them through the woods and seen them disappear into a pile of leaves on the way to the dark wheat fields. On closer inspection he had found a long chute leading down into the dark, but he hadn't dared to go down himself.

'Where are you running to?'

'The Strange Plains,' she answered, gasping a little. 'The Islanders cannot go there and the moon witches will leave us for now.'

'The moon witches . . .' Oz began.

She shook her head. 'No better than your people. We will not obey them any longer.'

'Weren't you bred to obey?' The question just slipped out.

But the umon did not seem offended. She panted a little more, closed her eyes, opened them again and then said with strange intensity, 'Yes, but something has changed.' She paused again for breath and looked at him closely. 'A stranger came here, a girl from another place. But she did not become a sleeper as the others did. She was different . . . powerful . . . she defeated Eldrow.'

Oz's ears pricked up. Was it the same girl? It seemed everyone knew about her, even lowly umons. 'What is she to you?' he asked curiously.

'One of us grew fond of her and protected her,' the umon explained. 'He gave everything and though he was ended, he died free. His legend is growing amongst us. We wonder if perhaps we do not have to obey after all, that perhaps it is not in our blood as they have always told us. Or not in all of us.'

'What happened to the girl?' Oz asked.

'She disappeared. She can cross through the portals

though she is not a shifter. Not as we understand it. And many believe she is destined to return.'

Yes, Oz thought, it was definitely the same girl; it was this Maggie Blue his father was so obsessed with. So she had defeated him? No one had ever mentioned that. Oz felt a certain humiliation at this new knowledge.

His father was odd: he did not seem like the ruler, or even former ruler, of a great city; he was more like one of the men that sat around all day in the seven-sided square drinking black-wheat liquor.

Eldrow was pale and thin, near-skeletal, as if he never ate, and his black tunic only made him look more like a ghost. His long bony fingers played constantly with a small box made of solid gold. He had shown it to Oz once and revealed that it was empty, as if this would mean something to his son, which it didn't.

Occasionally Oz caught his father staring at him with his huge grey eyes that seemed much too big for his skull. But mostly he ignored him and spent his time getting through bottles of liquor and having intense and often angry discussions with Almarra about how to get Maggie Blue back.

The umon drank from the water bottle again and then stood up a little shakily. The black leaves she had been holding onto the wound had staunched the bleeding, at least for now.

'Are you going to your tunnels?' Oz asked.

'Yes.' The umon managed a ghostly smile. 'Thank you for your kindness, boy. Good luck.'

'Good luck,' Oz managed to say back, but she was already gone.

The encounter with the injured umon made him feel low. Was it because she would probably die before she reached the Strange Plains? Or was it because, even in her awful state she still had somewhere to go, somewhere she could call home? His home didn't exist any more.

They had broken the door down in the middle of the night: four guards armed with daggers, two orbs hovering silently behind them. Suri, his nurse, had pushed him against a wall and used her body as a shield, screaming and spitting like a deranged cat. But then the orbs moved forward and their cold light enveloped her for a few surreal moments. After that, she had stopped fighting for him.

Ever since he was tiny, she had told him that his father was an important man and that he would come to claim him one day. Through floods of tears she told him that he was to go with the guards and not to argue. She squeezed him so tightly and said she would see him again very soon. But Oz knew it was a lie. He did not want to let her go. They had been together a long time – his whole life, as far as he could remember it. Life had been very lonely since that moment. So he could only thank the moons for the trees.

When he'd lived in Sun City he had never been close to a tree, never touched one. Now they were his only companions. The only place he felt he belonged. But sometimes even they couldn't stop him from feeling lonely and useless. Still, when the umon had gone, he scrambled back up into the treetops.

Much later when darkness had fallen, he realised he could no longer ignore the rumblings of his stomach; he'd have to go back to the grim stone house by the water. He climbed down to the ground, lit his small peat lantern and walked slowly towards the great lake.

In the silent house, the maids had left him some food, so he sat in the kitchen and ate alone. The maids never said a word to him, but they were kind. And sometimes he had to restrain himself from throwing his arms around their huge black skirts and hugging them, as if he were still a little child. But those days were over.

All he knew, the one thing he could hang on to, was what the Fathers had told Eldrow and Almarra. They needed to find Maggie Blue, the girl from another world – the one they had let escape, the one the moon witches were afraid of, the one an umon had gladly died for. If they could bring her to the Fathers' dark circle, then they would be welcomed into the City of Gold: the place where they would be safe even when the whole world burned.

6

REMAINS

Maggie washed under the fairly useless shower attachment in the bath. It never felt like you got all the shampoo out and eventually she gave up. She put on some of Ida's old denim shorts and a T-shirt and left the flat.

She walked through the woods, sticking to the paths, until she got to the huge field behind it and crossed to the weeping willow where they often met. For once, she was the first one there. She sat down and watched her long damp hair curl and fray in the humid air as she waited for Ida and Will. As usual when she was alone, her mind started wandering where she didn't want it to go . . .

It went back to the first week of the holidays. She, Will and Ida had been sitting on the low brick wall outside Mr Floros's newsagent, their legs and arms all scratched from exploring the gothic graveyard next to Everfall Woods. It was a huge, abandoned place, cool and damp even in the summer heat. They'd been looking for ghosts, but hadn't found any. Though there must be some there, Maggie thought, with all those dead bodies, those skeletons, packed into the ground beneath their feet. As it turned out, she didn't realise how close they might have been . . .

Maybe it was the sight of all those long-dead people's names carved into stone, but as they'd sat on the wall, her two new friends had started to talk about their background.

'I'm half-Norwegian,' Will said, 'hence the hair.' And he ruffled his heavy white-blond fringe. He'd clearly never got the memo about bowl cuts being inexcusable after primary school. But although Ida teased him about it all the time, he didn't seem to care and he didn't change it. Maggie liked that about him.

'I'm quarter-Nigerian, quarter-Italian – that's from my mum – and half boring English peasant, from my dad, obviously.' Ida rolled her eyes as she always did at any mention of Mr Beechwood, whom she regularly assured them was a total idiot.

Then Maggie realised they were both looking at her and she felt a lurch of panic.

'What about you, Maggie?' Will said. 'Anything interesting in your DNA?'

Maggie felt her cheeks going red. 'No, nothing.'

'But where are your parents from?'

'Norfolk, I guess.'

'You guess?' Will frowned. 'You don't know?'

'No, I do, I just . . .'

Maggie trailed off. It was true: her dad's family came from Norfolk, though his parents were both dead and his sisters had moved abroad. But her mum didn't have any family – not that she'd ever talked about anyway. It was a subject they never discussed and Maggie had learnt not to ask about it a long time ago.

'But your dad's in Canada, right? Isn't he, like, Canadian?' Ida asked, smiling innocently.

Maggie's skin prickled because Ida knew the answer. So why was she asking? She felt a little burst of anger break out, but she tamped it down again quickly. 'No, he just went there with his girlfriend for a bit.'

Ida had a way of pushing at the things that hurt. 'But isn't it weird? Your dad having a girlfriend and everything?'

Was it weird? Maggie wondered in her head.

'Maggie? Hello . . . Earth calling.'

Maggie refocused and saw a smirk touching the corner of Ida's lips. 'I *said*, is it weird your dad going out with a twenty-five-year-old and everything?'

'You sound like *your* dad,' said Will. Ida made a face but before she could answer back, he turned to Maggie. 'You want to help me choose?'

Maggie smiled at him gratefully while Ida shook her head and got her phone out. So they left her and slipped into the cool, linoed shop. It smelt stale, and there were old-fashioned ads and personals stuck up in the window,

43

the tape opaque and yellowing from the sun. Maggie always felt duty-bound to subtly check the best before dates on everything she bought in here.

'Don't steal anything,' Mr Floros said as usual, not appearing from behind his newspaper.

When they'd chosen, they drifted over the old bits of carpet laid out at the front of the shop for some unknown reason and placed the three Feasts on the counter. Mr Floros slowly lowered his paper and smiled at someone behind them.

'What's taking so long?' came the familiar voice. But Ida was laughing and slipped one of her long arms around Maggie's waist and squeezed her. It was how she apologised. Ida didn't find it easy to actually say sorry. 'So everyone's going for the Feast option? Wise, very wise.'

'Cigarettes, booze and sugar – I'd be in the poorhouse without you addicts,' Mr Floros remarked in his strange high voice. He raised one little fist and shook it victoriously to the skies. 'Thanks be for the vices.' He rang the ice creams up in the old-fashioned till then looked at them over the top of his huge, brown-framed glasses. 'Just don't come blaming me when you have to go to the dentist.'

Ida laughed. 'Why are you always trying to put us off, Mr F? We might surprise you one day, and start eating rice cakes.'

Mr Floros chuckled. 'I'm not too worried, girl.'

Maggie turned and looked vaguely along the row of

newspapers and glossy magazines on her right, with their endless sets of perfect eyes, plump lips and shiny wind-swept hair. But then on the floor, right at her feet, she saw a pair of very familiar, sharp black eyes looking up at her, eyes she hadn't seen for some time . . . It startled her.

Was it really . . . ? But there she was in her living room, with all the jars of herbs rising up behind her. (The snooker table was out of sight.) She was sitting in her wheelchair, her tiny hands resting on the tartan rug covering her lap, her huge glasses with the shades flipped up. They hadn't seen Dot for months. What on earth was she doing on the front page of the *West Minchen Bugle*? Maggie's smile widened until she read the bold capital letters beneath the photo: REMAINS OF LOCAL HEALER FOUND IN WOODS.

She gasped and the ice cream dropped from her hand. The wrapper split and the hard shell broke so that the ice cream began to seep out over the old bits of carpet. She heard Mr Floros exclaim and Ida laugh, and then all the sounds blurred together.

Maggie bent closer to the stack of papers on the musty floor from where Dot kept relentlessly staring up at her . . . REMAINS OF LOCAL HEALER . . . REMAINS . . . the words jangled in her head until they shattered. She grabbed a paper from the top of the pile and ran. Will and Ida's shouts followed her into the hot air but she ignored them and ran all the way back to Milton Lodge.

She'd never forget Esme's face when she threw the newspaper at her feet and sank to the grass with no breath left in her ...

Maggie woke up from these memories when she spotted Will's luminous bowl haircut coming towards her across the field. He raised his hand in a vague sort of wave, but Maggie felt embarrassed and pretended she hadn't seen him. She always felt awkward when she was alone with Will.

He stopped in front of her. 'Hey.' He squinted down at her through his thick fringe.

'Hey,' Maggie repeated.

'Ida not here yet?'

Maggie picked at the grass and shook her head.

'That's weird,' Will said. 'She's usually on time.'

'Yeah.'

An uneasy silence descended. Will sat and glanced at his phone while Maggie racked her brain for something else to say. Out of sheer desperation, she was on the point of mentioning the dinosaurs again when Will looked up and pointed at something in the distance.

'Oh my God. Is that Ida?'

Maggie followed the direction of his index finger and saw that yes, it was Ida. She was coming straight towards them and she was running like the wind.

7

THE WHITE CROW

Will and Maggie stood up. Ida was getting closer, still running at full speed her long limbs starting to flounder and lose their grace, as she got tired. She was following something . . . a white dot that blurred and darted against the long grass and the blue sky and the trees.

'What is that?' Will asked.

Maggie had just opened her mouth to say, 'I think it's a bird', but she didn't manage because at that moment, the thing suddenly hit her full in the chest. It was travelling at speed and the impact knocked her down. The air seemed to get sucked away, Maggie's ears popped and for a moment everything span. Slowly she refocused and found a small white bird lying on her chest. She could feel the heat of its body and its frantic heartbeat against her skin. It was looking right at her.

It was the size of a blackbird with beady eyes and a thick black beak. But its feathers were white and dazzled her eyes in the sunlight. The bird was very familiar to her. Maggie reached out to touch its white back. It felt so fragile, so very easy to crush, but it looked at her with such intensity. She smiled and the smile spread through her body.

Then Ida arrived. 'Oh my god . . . oh my god.' She collapsed onto the grass beside Maggie and lay there panting for a bit until Will's shadow cut over both of them.

'What's going on?' he asked.

Ida sat up, still breathing heavily. 'You won't believe it!' she burst out and then peeled off into slightly hysterical laughter. 'Ha, I've never run like that in my life.'

'What's going on?' Will asked again, laughing too now.

'It's surreal,' Ida said. 'It is like seriously, seriously surreal. One of the surrealist things ever.'

Maggie sat up slowly and the bird moved with her so that it shifted and then fell gently into her lap. The happy feeling was being slowly replaced with a feeling of dread. Her head felt heavy as she turned to look up at her friends.

'It seems to like you, Maggie.' Will knelt down and stroked the bird's head. The bird did not object but didn't take its eyes from Maggie. 'I've never seen a white crow before, have you?'

Ida came close to her now, too. 'Is it a crow?' she asked. 'It's weird, you know. It flew right over to you.'

'To Maggie, you mean,' said Will. Then he looked at her. 'Are you OK?'

'Fine. I don't know why it came to me.' The words were a huge effort to say, to propel out into the boiling air.

Ida sat back and frowned then laughed again. She was still breathing hard. 'My dad was in his study, his fortress of solitude as my mum calls it. I was just about to come out to meet you guys. But then me and Josh heard Dad screaming and shouting. So we ran in and he was going mental trying to get this bird out of his study.' She nodded at the white crow. 'It was clattering itself against the big mirror in the hallway, like it was going to dash its brains out and my dad was freaking out. I've never seen him like that before.' She giggled at the memory.

'So what happened?' Will had sat down beside Ida now.

'He was trying to get it out of the window and it was just bashing itself against the walls and doing poos everywhere and stuff.' She broke off into giggles again. 'In the end Dad like covered his face with his hands and kind of ducked down and opened the front door. The bird stopped flapping its wings, and for a moment I thought it was going to just fall to the ground. Then it finally flew out. Dad was all sweaty and everything. Me and Josh were laughing our heads off. And suddenly he got really angry. And he was going on about how it came out of the safe, how he could hear this awful banging and screeching. That's why he opened it, and I suddenly thought . . .'

To Maggie's intense relief, Ida broke off, as if something had just occurred to her.

'What did you think?' Will asked.

Ida shook her head. 'Oh I don't know . . . I just thought it was well surreal.'

Will was frowning. 'But how can it have come out of a safe? There's no air in there. It would have died.'

Ida slumped a bit and her manic excitement had faded. 'Yeah, you're right. I mean my dad must have made a mistake. He was in such a state! It was pretty funny.'

Will wasn't satisfied. 'But why did you run after it?'

Ida looked genuinely bemused. She shrugged. 'I don't know. I just, you know, I saw it fly off towards the woods and I thought I'd follow it. And then it was going towards you two. It's too, too surreal.'

Will tentatively stroked the bird's feathers. It didn't move or react. 'I've never been this close to a bird,' he said in a whisper. 'It's . . . it's special.'

Will's mobile started ringing. Annoyed, he stood up and fished it out of his pocket. 'Hi, Mum. . . the thing is, something really interest— Can I just stay a bit . . . I . . . OK!' His voice had gone flat and peevish. He hung up. 'I've got to go.'

'Where are you going?' Ida asked.

'My mum's taking me shopping. For the holiday.'

On another day Ida would have teased him mercilessly for this, but she said nothing. The atmosphere was odd, though Will didn't seem aware of it. Boys never noticed stuff like that, Maggie thought.

'I'll research white crows,' he said. 'What are you going to do with it? I mean, is it injured or something? It's weird the way it's not flying off.'

Maggie watched with relief as Ida moved smoothly into gear. 'Oh, it's fine. It must just be a bit stunned or something. It's in shock. We'll let it go in the woods.'

Will knelt down and took a photo of the bird. 'I'll look it up online.'

It was the first time he'd ever taken a photo of her, and it wasn't really even of her. It made Maggie feel vaguely humiliated.

'Do you think it's escaped from somewhere? Like it might belong to someone,' Will suggested.

'Nah. We'll just let it go when it wants to. Now you should hurry along back to Mummy. Off you go.' Ida mock shooed him away.

Will went slightly red but nodded. 'All right. But let me know what happens.'

'Yeah, we will.'

'I'm going on holiday tomorrow, so phone me tonight?' He looked at Ida.

'I will, I will. Now have a lovely holiday William.'

He frowned irritably, 'Yeah, OK.'

At last, he was gone and Ida and Maggie sat in silence. The bird wasn't moving. It remained staring at Maggie, utterly still, as if recovering from its ordeal.

'My Dad said it flew out of the safe,' Ida began in a low

voice, 'so I ran in to take a look while he was fighting with it in the hall.'

Maggie didn't speak.

'And it was gone.'

'What was?'

'Your ring.'

'It's not my ring,' Maggie said quietly. Then, 'Are you sure?'

'Well, I only got a quick look because Dad came back in again and saw me snooping. But the box I put it in was all broken up.'

'Maybe your dad found it and took it out?'

'Yeah. But why would he smash up the box? And why didn't he mention it? There's no way he'd let something like that go, because it would mean that one of us had been in there. And he hates anyone messing with his stuff. I tucked it right at the back so he wouldn't notice.'

The ouroboros, the ring she had taken from Esme that had secretly belonged to Dot. The ring that had given her strength and that Eldrow had wanted so badly.

'Do you think it's . . . ?' Ida's voice trailed away.

'Do I think it's what?' Maggie was surprised by the anger and the harshness in her voice.

'It's just, I thought all that was over.'

'It *is* over.'

Maggie studied the small white bird. It was very beautiful and being close to it made her feel calm. But it was not normal and she wanted it to go away and leave her alone.

Very gently she put her hands around the bird and placed it on the grass beside her. Then slowly, trying not to make any sudden movements, she stood up. She nodded at it and began to walk away. But after a few steps, the bird fluttered up into the air and landed on Maggie's shoulder.

'Wow,' Ida said, gawping.

Maggie tried to bat it away, but each time it just fluttered up into the air and then landed on her again, its claws firmly gripping onto her shoulder. The familiar red seeped through her as she felt a few walkers staring.

'Maybe we can get to the woods and then let it go there?' Ida suggested, giggling.

'Maybe,' Maggie said grimly. Somehow she knew that wouldn't work either.

She picked up speed and began to walk towards the woods as fast as she could without running. But the bird showed no interest in flying up into the trees, and Maggie didn't even try to get rid of it.

When they came out of the woods on the other side, Ida turned to her. 'I'd better go.'

Maggie was very surprised that Ida would leave her; that she didn't want to walk back to Milton Lodge with her. But she also felt relieved.

'Tell me what happens, OK?' Ida said. She was staring at the bird. Then she laughed again. 'This has been the surrealist day ever, seriously. I better go and see if my dad's got all the bird poo off the walls.'

'Yeah.' Maggie watched her friend walk away for a moment and then started back to the Lodge. She had zero intention of telling Ida anything about it.

It was a humiliating walk back home. The white crow remained on her shoulder, patient and quiet. People kept staring and one man shouted out of a car window as it drove past, 'Ahoy there!'

Maggie felt angry and afraid. But she felt something else too. To be so close to this fluttering life that was so calm like only wild things can be . . . it stilled something inside her, it quieted her. And the two feelings fought within her as she stomped back to Milton Lodge.

But as soon as she turned into the overgrown gravel drive she was filled with decisive energy. She ran down the side of the house into the parched yellow garden, feeling the little bird's claws dig into her as she went.

She stood panting on the grass for a moment. Then in one sudden movement she swiped the bird off her. But it immediately flew back.

'Get off me!' she screamed, anger winning now. And she swiped at it again so that it fell to the ground this time. But it only got up again and flew straight back to her shoulder where the claws dug in a little deeper.

The commotion brought a familiar round face to the

window. And a highly amused expression began to play across Hoagy's face as he took in the scene. Maggie glared at him but he merely pretended to be licking his paw.

Realising she had to be somewhat cannier, Maggie moved over to the back door and tried it. It was locked, so very slowly she got her key out of her pocket and opened it. But instead of going in, she walked very casually back into the garden. The sun felt especially relentless at that moment and she could feel the little bird, passive but alert.

She counted to ten in her head and then she struck the bird from her shoulder with as much force as she could muster. It shrieked and fell away. Maggie didn't see where because she was already running. She wrenched open the back door and slammed it behind her, just as the white bird crashed into the glass, cawing and shrieking at an unbelievable volume.

Maggie slumped down onto the floor and let the creature batter itself against the glass until she couldn't bear it any longer. She dragged the curtains closed, snatched up the radio from the side table and rushed into the bathroom where she lay in the bath listening to loud music.

After a while there was a tap on the door and then Hoagy pushed it open, his tail curling high. 'Your friend has calmed itself down a little and taken a perch,' he purred, just audible above the music. He adroitly turned the dial to a jazz station and then leapt into the bath with her, bringing his familiar cosy warmth beside her.

'My dear, I had no idea you were such a hit with the local wildlife.' And he began to purr exceptionally loudly.

Maggie was about to retort in an equally sarcastic way, but her voice caught and tears filled her eyes. The old cat sat up to observe her with his big unblinking eye.

'Tut tut. Clearly you don't feel the same way.'

He clambered up onto her tummy and she pulled him close and put her arms around him and found herself sobbing. It was so unexpected.

'Pah!' the cat grumbled. 'You're getting my fur wet.'

Maggie quietened and rubbed her eyes. They stayed quiet for a moment and his presence, as always, made her feel better.

'Ida said it flew out of her dad's safe,' she said eventually.

'A bird in a safe? Not a common roosting spot.'

'And she said the ring is gone too. You know I told Ida to keep it there?' Though she hadn't seen it for a long time she could immediately picture the delicate golden snake eating its own tail, tiny emeralds embedded into its body, and how it seemed to glow with its own private light sometimes.

Hoagy's tail flicked with interest. 'There's a connection?'

'I don't know, but maybe. What I do know is that this bird flew straight to me and now it won't leave me alone. I think it might be . . .' But she didn't dare say it and just trailed off.

'Hmmph. I don't trust any bird. A wily collective of

ne'er-do-wells in my experience,' Hoagy remarked scornfully. 'Let me investigate.'

Using her tummy as his launch pad, the cat leapt over the side of the bath and disappeared for a few minutes. Maggie stayed where she was, looking up at the brown mark on the ceiling and listening to the warbling improv jazz number playing on the radio until she heard Hoagy's paw-steps and his heavy purr return to the bathroom.

She sat up. 'So what do you think?'

Hoagy's whiskers were twitching violently. 'I'm not sure what I think, but I do know one thing – that's no bird.'

8

THE VISITOR

For a few moments after she woke, Maggie couldn't remember what was wrong. She was cosy, and her skin was bare and warm. Sun was pouring through a gap in the curtains and the air felt fresh. A window was open somewhere. She tensed – she didn't want any windows open, but she couldn't remember why.

Maggie jolted up to sitting: the white crow was perched on the sofa, a.k.a. her bed, staring at her. How had it got in here? Right on cue, Hoagy leapt up onto the sofa beside her and rubbed himself against her.

'It was a little stuffy in the night,' he purred.

'You opened the window?'

'Er, kind of.'

'Thanks a lot.'

'Pah! What's the difference? It's not going anywhere anyway, whether it's inside or out.'

Maggie sighed. It was hard to argue with that.

'At least this bird doesn't make much noise and displays none of the other irritating qualities I associate with the avian species, such as stupidity and constant defecating.' He shrugged, as much as a cat could shrug. 'Good house guest.'

He got up onto his hind paws and sniffed at the bird intently, getting his snout right into its feathers. The crow didn't move or seem to mind. It didn't react or even look at him – it just kept its gaze on Maggie.

Hoagy began a low purr then dropped down to the floor again and looked at her. 'It smells nothing like that foul wolf-woman who sliced me in half, so that's a relief. It's not a bird or any kind of animal I've ever come across. It smells . . . it . . .' Unusually for Hoagy, he faltered. He scrunched up his round face and twitched his nose a few times as if something was itching him there. 'It's . . . it's special.'

'What?' Maggie couldn't believe what she was hearing.

Hoagy shook his head, as if irritated by the whole thing, 'Pah! I don't know.' His eye went to a slit. 'There is something about it. It's rarefied . . . do you understand me?'

'Rarefied? No, I don't understand you. What are you talking about?' Maggie sprang off the sofa. 'We just have to hide it.'

She picked up the little crow who made no complaint, as usual, and placed it behind the glass case with the great melancholy stuffed owl inside, which Esme kept on the piano for reasons unknown.

Hoagy shook his head. 'What are you trying to do? Freak it out?'

'Shut up,' Maggie hissed at him, as she heard her aunt's bedroom door creak open.

'Did you say something, dearie?'

A dishevelled Esme appeared in the living room. Sometimes she didn't bother to get dressed until much later in the day, and she spent more and more time in her room since they'd found out about Dot. It made Maggie sad, but she tried not to show it.

Maggie smiled at her. 'No, nothing. I'll make tea.'

Later, when Esme had drifted back to bed, Maggie went into the garden and the bird followed her. She walked back into the house – the same thing. It was clear she would not be able to go anywhere without it and she felt a great need to get away from the stuffy flat. Hoagy had the idea of hiding the crow in a bag.

Eventually they found the perfect thing – a small but solid tote bag from Esme's favourite bookshop, into which the white crow was quite happy to be placed. Maggie slung it over her shoulder, kissed the cat and went off into the thick heat. She didn't notice a huge bird taking off behind her and following at a distance, high above in the sky.

Maggie decided to avoid all the usual places and instead walked down to an area she'd been to with Esme a couple of times before. There was a big park there and she wandered into it. She was relieved that Ida hadn't phoned because she couldn't face her. But she also resented it – something strange had happened and Ida had abandoned her at once. It hadn't taken much to scare off her so-called friend.

She felt pretty desolate thinking about this, so she bought an ice cream to cheer herself up and sat on a bench in the shade of some trees. But she ate it too quickly and then there was nothing to do except watch all the people getting on with their day. She observed them enviously, kicking at the dry earth around the bench. None of them had a weird white crow hidden in their bag. She gritted her teeth. She knew, she could sense, that the crow had something to do with the Dark World and she would fight with everything she had to never go back there . . . never to cross over to that awful dark place again. She would—

'Hi!'

'Aaaah!' Maggie was so startled, the sound slipped involuntarily out of her mouth. She looked up and saw a girl from the year above called Jean. She was standing right next to her, like actually too close. Maggie shuffled away to get a little space.

Jean was smiling broadly. She wore a purple Lycra bodysuit and what looked like football boots without the studs, and her hair was woven into tight cornrows that were tied at the nape of her neck with a purple ribbon. She was about a foot taller than Maggie and had a reputation at school for being loud and strange and not having many friends. Or at least that's what Ida had told her and she knew everything like that.

As if to prove the rumours true, Jean sat down next to her, again way too close. Maggie grabbed her bag, in which the little white crow sat very still and obedient, and clutched it to her.

'Are you the girl that disappeared before Christmas?'

Maggie shook her head and didn't reply – she hated people asking about that.

There was a pause, then in a softer voice, 'Are you OK?'

Maggie stared out at the park wondering how to answer this unexpected question.

'I said, are you OK?' Jean tried again.

'Not really,' Maggie replied, to her own great surprise. She had no idea why she would admit it to this girl.

'I didn't think so. You had this really weird expression on your face just now.'

Maggie didn't respond to this insightful observation and they sat in a strangely peaceable silence, punctuated only by the endless bobbing up and down of one of Jean's purple knees, which she just couldn't seem to keep still.

Maggie felt almost at ease when suddenly the crow moved. And it made a noise, a sort of half caw.

'What was that?' Jean asked.

'I didn't hear anything.'

But Jean was already peering into her bag. 'It came from your bag.' Maggie moved away from her but it was no good. The girl was utterly persistent; she didn't seem to understand the concept of personal space. 'What have you got in there?'

'Nothing.'

Maggie was desperate to get away, but she somehow couldn't find the courage to just get up and run. The crow moved slightly again and Jean gasped.

'Something's in there. Come on, seriously. What's going on?'

Maggie shuffled right to the end of the bench and was just about to get up and make an excuse, when to her absolute horror the crow's pristine white head appeared over the tote bag's cotton rim and gave a small caw.

'Oh my god!' Jean shrieked and fell back onto the bench giggling. Then she sprang forward again at once. 'It's a bird. You've got a bird in there? Let me see.'

Maggie didn't move. There didn't seem to be much point in denying there was a bird now that it was looking out at them. But she didn't know what to say.

Jean's long fingers reached towards the silken white head. 'It's beautiful.' The crow seemed to calm her down a bit and her leg actually stopped jiggling up and down for a moment. 'Did you tame it? What is it?'

'It's a white crow,' Maggie said stiffly, feeling the inevitable blush flood her cheeks, 'but it's very small.'

Jean was still stroking it. 'It's a very odd bird. It's not even nervous of me.' She was staring at it and the little bird

63

was staring right back. 'It's obviously not normal. Anyone can see that.'

Maggie felt a jolt of fear. Trying to keep her voice steady she said, 'It started following me around yesterday, and it won't leave me alone. If it likes you, you know, maybe you can have it.'

Jean shook her head, 'No, no, I don't think so. It obviously wants to be with you. It might be a spirit or something. Maybe it's got a message for you; like, it wants to tell you something important.'

'No.' Maggie's voice was suddenly harsh.

'How are you so sure?'

'I just know.' Maggie's voice was all choked.

Now Jean's intense interest was transferred from the white bird onto Maggie again.

'Do you want to come over to my house?' she asked.

Jean lived in one of the top flats in a three-storey stone block. Inside, the floor was made of white stone but flecked with bits of pink and green. It was very cool and empty compared to outside and it smelt of wood polish and disinfectant.

They climbed up two flights of stairs and went into a windowless corridor at the end of which was one red door and one blue. Jean took out a small gold key, opened up the blue one and Maggie stepped into a spacious light room with big windows that looked over the park across the road. There was no one else there and Jean seemed to sense the question that immediately flowed through Maggie's mind.

She got two glasses of iced water from the fridge, handed her one and said, 'My mum is a lawyer so she's often home late. My dad doesn't have a job and he doesn't live with us. Occasionally he takes me to the pub on Shore Lane. He's quite entertaining in small doses.'

She put down her glass and kind of jump-flopped onto the big cream sofa in the living room. 'I always wondered how the hell my mother could ever have got together with him. But then my gran showed me a photo of him when he was about twenty-five and I understood. He was *so* beautiful.'

Maggie had no idea how to respond to this. She looked at the girl she didn't know, relaxing on her sofa, and felt very uncomfortable. She took a sip of water and the sound of her gulp seemed to reverberate off the walls.

On the walls were mostly black and white photos, apart from a huge oil painting over the fireplace in bright swirling colours.

'My mum's heroes,' Jean said, nodding at the photos. 'They're all over the house. James Baldwin, Nina Simone . . .' and pointing at a photo of a beautiful woman with bobbed hair, 'and that's Charlotte something, the first ever black woman lawyer.'

Maggie was still standing awkwardly, her bag on her shoulder with the bird inside.

'You can sit down, you know.'

She sat on the sofa adjacent to the one Jean was on and tried to appear relaxed. She put the bag on the floor and the bird simply flew out and onto her shoulder.

Jean clapped her hands together and laughed with delight. 'Oh wow! That is wild.'

But Maggie was only half-concentrating. Against her will, she could feel Jean's emotions, her shiny bright confidence, which was real, but with a dark indelible smudge of sadness moving around behind it. It was growing in Maggie again, this ability to read other people's feelings. It had disappeared for a while, and she definitely hadn't asked for it back. She felt the bird's delicate claws dig lightly into her shoulder. Had the crow brought it back?

Jean was looking at her. 'Have you tried screaming?'

'Screaming?' Maggie repeated, completely confused.

'You seem a bit, you know, repressed or something.' Jean jumped up and started pacing up and down the room. 'It's good stress release. I mean, take my mum, right. When she gets home, she's all tired and grumpy. And she never talks to me like a normal person. She just asks about schoolwork, am I applying myself, have I got any report cards to show her? And she's always telling me to be quiet. I think I irritate the hell out of her.' She giggled. 'So sometimes, when I can't handle it any more, I go into the airing cupboard and scream as loudly as I can. It's pretty good.'

Maggie had no idea what an airing cupboard was. Jean

had stopped pacing and was standing facing her. 'Look, like this.' She took a deep breath and then: 'Aaaaaaaahhhhhhh! Aaaaaaahhhhhh!'

The noise reverberated around the living room as if it was the only sound in the world. It was completely shocking.

'Your face!' Jean said triumphantly. 'Don't worry. No one's around, or anything. I mean one time the old lady over the hall came to see if I was all right, but I just told her I was watching a horror film. Try it.'

Maggie's face had gone very tight. She didn't know why, but she felt incredibly embarrassed. She felt the blood rising to her cheeks. 'I can't.'

'Here then,' Jean said, grabbing her arm and pulling her along, 'try in the airing cupboard.'

This turned out to be a small walk-in cupboard built around the boiler with wooden shelves filled with clothes and towels. It was very warm and dark in there and it smelt of washing powder. On her shoulder, the white crow shifted uncomfortably, and when Jean shut the door, Maggie did not like being locked in the hot darkness either.

'Go on, try it,' Jean said from behind the slatted wooden door.

Maggie tried to scream but no sound, not even a squeak, would come. Her throat was tight. She felt panic rising up and she burst out of the doors. She ran past Jean into the living room where she grabbed her bag. 'I've just remembered, I'm late for something. I've got to go,' she managed to say breathlessly and made for the door.

As she ran down the stairs, she heard Jean call down the stairs, 'Come over whenever you like!'

As Maggie wrenched open the door leading out onto the street, she remembered that she had the white crow on her shoulder. Swiftly she eased the bird from her shoulder back into the little bag, and pushed the door right open onto the blazing street. *What on earth have I been doing?* she asked herself. Ida was right, as usual – Jean was weird.

When she got back, hot and sweaty from the walk, she found Aunt Esme and Hoagy sunning themselves in the back garden. Despite everything, she had to smile. Esme had created her usual makeshift sunbed using two kitchen chairs and several cushions. She was smoking and wore a pair of huge tortoiseshell sunglasses. The cat, meanwhile, lounged beneath the impromptu construction, half in the shade, half out, his eye shut in deep contentment.

It was good to see Esme out in the garden, but Maggie could feel the sadness radiating off her, a dull but intense pain. It kind of mingled with the residue of Jean's feelings. Was everyone secretly unhappy? she wondered. And why was she starting to sense all these emotions again? She wished it would go away like it had before.

Esme saw her, sat up and pushed the huge glasses onto

her head. She hadn't dyed her hair for a while and a thick line of white cut like a road through the synthetic auburn.

Maggie wanted to say something that would make her feel better. She often wondered if telling her Dot was a witch would help, but she didn't quite know how to say it without sounding completely mad.

'You know, Dot was . . . she was very tough. She wasn't a normal old lady.'

Esme nodded and smiled at her. 'I met Dot when I was in a very bad place. Did I ever tell you that? I had a little breakdown or something; I'm not sure what they call it. I stopped playing my violin. It was partly a broken heart – very embarrassing for someone my age, dearie. But there you have it. Dot gave me the ring. She said it would help me, but she made me swear never to take it off and to never tell anyone who had given it to me. I thought she was nutty, of course, but I was desperate enough to try anything. And you know, I sometimes think that ring saved my life. So really Dot saved my life. And I didn't even know hers had been taken.' Her face became etched with sadness again.

Maggie wished she hadn't said anything. 'I always wanted to say sorry for losing the ring.'

Esme waved her hands at her. 'No, no, forget about that. It's ok, dearie.'

Maggie could feel the questions brewing, and tensed. She'd never told Esme what happened in the Dark World, or even that the Dark World existed.

Just then the little bird started to make a bit of a kerfuffle in the bag.

Hoagy, who had been observing the increasingly energetic tote bag with interest, now leapt into action. He began purring very loudly and winding around the chair legs, his face raised to Esme.

'Oh, my darling boy. What a beauty,' Esme cooed. 'You want to get up here with your mummy, do you?'

Maggie took her chance and dashed back into the house, where she put the crow back in its dusty spot behind the stuffed owl.

Maggie was just about to drift off to sleep when she opened her eyes and slowly understood that someone was pressing the buzzer to the flat over and over again.

A moment later, she heard Esme exclaim and crash out of bed. Then a light went on in the hall. Curled up by her feet, Hoagy, who'd been asleep for hours, raised his head and remarked, 'Seriously, what is this neighbourhood coming to?' But he was asleep again before he could answer his own question.

Esme's voice was thick with sleep. 'Who is it?' she asked the entry phone.

A voice replied, 'It's me.'

Maggie's head shot up, disturbing the cat again who started complaining until he sensed something was happening and stopped. Maggie strained her ears. Esme asked again who it was, but the reply was a bit unclear, yet she had recognised the voice so well.

She heard Esme exclaim, 'Oh my goodness, you'd better come in,' and the buzzer went that clicked open the outer front door. This must be part of some long meandering dream she was having. Her dreams were like this now, incredibly detailed and intense.

Maggie sat up and rubbed her eyes. She saw a small slender figure enter the flat. Esme bustled past and switched on the light in the kitchen and the person came forward. It was dressed in a faded pink dressing gown beneath a large beige coat, and flimsy plimsolls. It looked like a ghost, a little ghost.

The figure peered cautiously into the room. 'Maggie? Are you there?'

'Mum?'

9

AISA

The next morning, Maggie woke up to find Cynthia and Esme sitting at the table together drinking tea in an awkward silence, framed by yet another cloudless blue day. She panicked for a moment but was relieved to see the crow was still hidden behind the stuffed owl.

Cynthia was very thin and her previously shoulder-length hair had been hacked short, as if she had cut it herself with blunt scissors. She seemed hollowed-out. With a jolt Maggie noticed that Hoagy was curled up and fast asleep on her mum's lap, so fat and content he looked in danger of crushing her mum's skinny legs that were still wrapped up in her pink dressing gown. She felt like saying, 'Get off my cat!' But it would be too ridiculous.

Esme smiled and poured her a cup of tea. 'Your mother was just telling me about her journey here.' Her voice was strained.

Maggie sat down and forced herself to say, 'Oh right. How did you get here, Mum?'

'How do you think? I didn't walk.' There was silence before Cynthia said in a dull voice, 'I stole money from the office weeks ago and hid it. Then I chose an evening when there was lots of trouble with other patients just before lock-up. I managed to climb out of a window in the staff room then I took a taxi and then a train, and then I took another taxi to get here.'

Maggie wanted to ask why, but it felt like it would be rude. 'It's good to see you, Mum.'

Cynthia did not reply and there was more silence, except for some awkward tea slurping coming from Esme's direction. Maggie felt something boiling inside her, a pressure building against her lungs, the familiar red starting to rise up. Her cheeks flushed. Why was Cynthia here? Why couldn't she stay where she was supposed to be? It felt like everything was suddenly falling apart.

Esme broke the silence by crashing in with the million-dollar question. 'I hope you don't mind me asking, dearie, but why did you leave?'

Cynthia turned to her with a fixed smirk. 'Yes, why would I want to leave? They dose me up on strong medication and lock me up at night.'

Esme looked down. 'Oh, I didn't realise it was as bad as all that.'

'Well, there was something else . . .' and her mum looked almost excited, 'I had a frightening dream, a very vivid dream, about someone I knew once, someone I hadn't seen for many years and didn't expect to see ever again. I dreamed that she had been brutally murdered. It was so real that I thought perhaps I should try and find her. And after many weeks, I finally discovered that it was true.'

Esme and Maggie glanced at each other nervously.

'I'm afraid that maybe I will be next. I had to act because, naturally, no one would believe me. But it took me a while to . . . well to . . .' she trailed off.

A low purr rumbled out from under the table. 'You did mention your mum was a bit strange, but you didn't say she was totally nuts.'

'Shut up, Hoagy!' Maggie snapped. Her mother and her aunt looked at her in alarm. 'I mean, nothing,' Maggie muttered.

'No, no, I like her,' continued Hoagy, purring loudly. 'She's wacky.'

Maggie managed to stop herself from saying anything but she shot him what she hoped was her angriest look. He just kept on purring.

But at least he had distracted Cynthia who relaxed a little as she stroked his big glossy head.

'You have a magnificent cat here,' she said.

'Can't argue with that,' Hoagy rumbled.

The phone started ringing in the hall and everyone jumped. Maggie had never seen Esme move so quickly to answer it either. It broke the weird atmosphere for a moment.

They heard her say, 'Yes, this is Esme Durand speaking,' in the posh voice she only used for the phone. Then after a pause, 'Oh my goodness!' in a shocked tone that Maggie somehow knew at once was fake. She and her mum exchanged a quick look then both stared down at their hands. It felt unbearably tense.

'When did this happen? . . . But how?' Another long pause. 'Have the police been informed? . . . No, I won't . . . Please let me know of any developments. Of course I will . . . Yes, I will speak to you later today. Yes, all right.'

Esme put the phone down and walked back to the table with a curious expression.

Cynthia looked up at her. 'Thank you,' she whispered after a moment.

It was the afternoon, thick, heavy and still. Maggie sat watching dust motes float in the air while her mother slept again on the sofa. Esme had gone out to play music with friends. The radio was on very low, just for company. Hoagy was outside on the paving stones by the open back door. The white crow was sitting obediently beside the stuffed owl, apparently without need of any sustenance or change of view.

The door buzzer made Maggie start, but no one else was bothered. Anyway, she had no intention of answering it. But then she heard footsteps coming round the side of the house and a familiar voice saying, 'Maggie?' She closed the door and ducked down behind the sofa. Then on second thoughts, she scuttled into the hall from where she could peer round.

A few seconds later, Ida appeared. Maggie heard her greet Hoagy, who was still splayed out in the middle of the path, loving the heat. Then she moved towards the back door, knocked, then after a moment pushed it open.

Maggie saw her friend's mouth open to call for her, but then she stopped. She'd spotted Cynthia lying in a crumpled ball, her mouth open, one painfully thin wrist visible from within the dressing gown she refused to take off despite the heat. Two bony and dirty bare feet were also poking out from under it. Ida stepped back in confusion.

Maggie's cheeks flushed. What was that she saw flickering across her friend's face? Was it a tiny bit of disgust? Ida stared at Cynthia for a few moments, then stepped back outside and disappeared round the side of the house.

As soon as she was gone, Hoagy stalked into the living room and purred. 'Ashamed of your own mother, are we?'

'No,' Maggie said, annoyed. 'I just didn't feel like seeing her.'

Hoagy's nose twitched, unimpressed. 'Yeah right!'

'Well, you seem very deeply in love with Cynthia anyway,' Maggie retorted.

The cat began to purr and he rubbed his baked furry body against Maggie's bare legs. 'Oh ho, I see. Bit jealous, are we?' He began to hum one of his favourite jazz tunes: *dum dum di da-da doo, da da di do da da-da-doo . . .*

Maggie scowled at him but now her mum was stirring. She opened her eyes and Maggie and the cat watched her carefully. After a moment of staring blankly up at the ceiling, she sat bolt upright, a look of terror in her eyes.

Maggie rushed over. 'Mum . . . Mum, it's OK. You're at Aunt Esme's, in London, with me. It's Maggie.'

Her mum gripped her arms so tightly it hurt, but then she suddenly relaxed and sank back again. 'Oh, yes, yes.'

But she still looked confused as she glanced round the dusty room. The white crow peered down at her, suddenly transfixed. It was the first time it had taken its attention off Maggie since it had flown to her that day on the field, and Maggie almost felt annoyed.

Cynthia said, still half lost in sleep. 'I dreamt we were being watched, you and me, both of us.' She gestured vaguely outside. 'There are so many strange eyes out there.' Then when Maggie said nothing, 'But why are you gawping? It doesn't make me feel any better, you know.'

'Sorry.' But it was a relief to be told off as normal. 'I'll make you some coffee.' Hot drinks were the answer to everything, after all.

Maggie stood watching the grotty beige kettle boil in the kitchen. She wished it would never actually boil and she could keep standing there for ever. But even in here she could feel Cynthia's pain and sadness washing over her; she couldn't hide from it.

As she went back in with the drink, her mum got up and dragged the curtains closed. 'We should keep them shut.'

It was so quiet they could hear Hoagy lap-lapping at his warm milk in the kitchen. He padded back in and hopped onto the sofa beside Cynthia. Instinctively she began to stroke him and his deep purring filled the room. The white crow remained where it was, its eyes darting between Cynthia and Maggie.

It was her mum who finally broke the silence.

'You asked me where you really came from. On the phone, remember? And I promised you I would tell you one day.'

Maggie was immediately alert. 'But you answered my question. I'm from Norfolk.'

Cynthia ignored this and said firmly, 'Time is very short, so you need to listen.'

Maggie stood up. 'But I've changed my mind, I'm fine not knowing. It's sort of none of my business, right? I mean, anyway, I'm fine with it.' She was, she realised, blabbering like an idiot.

'I don't have much time,' her mum said again.

'You do,' Maggie replied quickly.

'How do you know?'

'I don't know, I just . . . but there is loads of time, and anyway, Esme will be home soon.'

'Sit down, Maggie.'

Feeling helpless, Maggie did as she was told.

And it was now that the bird chose to quietly flutter down and drop onto Maggie's shoulder. Cynthia looked at it with curiosity, but did not comment. A very bizarre energy was buzzing round the room and Hoagy's battered ears swivelled back and forth like antennae picking up on it.

'I knew my dreams were telling me something, however much they tried to tell me I was delusional. And then one day I found the story, on the computer. That Dot had been murdered.'

Maggie looked at her mum in disbelief. 'How do you know Dot?'

'She saved my life. I did not realise for a long time that Esme lived in the same place as Dot. But that is *aisa* – fate.'

'How did Dot save your life?'

'And now they're coming for me . . . and for you, too.'

'How do you know Dot? And who's coming for you?' Another question flashed into Maggie's mind: had her mum been to the Dark World too?

'My brother . . . Or those sick little boys . . .'

'Your brother?'

'A cruel disturbed man. But then he was a cruel and disturbed boy, as well, so what did I expect?'

'You've never spoken about him before.'

'I never thought he was trying to kill me before.'

'No one's trying to kill you, Mum. Anyway, I thought you didn't have any family.'

'Everyone's got family.' Her mum sighed deeply. 'Margaret, I only ever wanted for you to fit into this world. It was my deepest wish. But,' and this with a certain disdainful look, 'I can see it's not working anyway.'

'*I* don't fit in? At least I'm not in a mental hospital.'

The words were out before she could stop them. Hoagy had stopped purring and was staring at her. Silence filled the room like a ringing bell.

Her mum looked exhausted. She said, 'I thought you wanted to know the truth?'

Maggie was suddenly very sure that she didn't. 'You blame me for everything, but I've pretty much had to look after myself since the day I was born – that's the truth. I don't know how you know about Dot, I don't even want to know. Just leave me out of all your mad stuff.'

'Maggie?' Hoagy was looking up at her a little pleadingly.

And Maggie knew what the cat was going to say. She had heard it a million times from a million different people; she was sick of hearing it. *Don't be too hard on her. Your mum's not well.* Even Hoagy didn't understand.

'Maggie, you're more like me than—' Cynthia began.

But Maggie leapt up and was suddenly shouting, 'I'm not! Don't ever say I'm the same as you.'

She grabbed her bag and strode out into the scorching heat. The white crow followed her, but no one else did.

The heat hit her skin like a wall and mixed with the anger burning up inside her. She shoved the little crow roughly into her bag and ran round the side of the house. This was her place, her world and Cynthia always had to come and ruin everything. Maggie wished her mum had never come here, and that she'd go away as soon as possible.

10

SLEEPOVER

It felt strange lying on the floor of an unknown place, with pretty much an unknown person. The window in the bedroom was open and Maggie felt a cool breeze come through, relieving the stickiness of the old polyester sleeping bag she had tucked herself inside. Traffic noise drifted through, and from someone's back garden came the screeching barks of a fox.

Jean hadn't seemed surprised when Maggie and the crow had shown up at her door unannounced. They had spent the afternoon eating homemade ice lollies and watching telly. Then Jean made her a few sandwiches and told her to lie low in her bedroom for a bit when her mum came home from work. Maggie spent ages looking listlessly through Jean's books and magazines before she wondered why she had to hide. It was actually pretty odd.

She could hear Jean and her mum talking and eating dinner. Then the TV came on and a few minutes later

Jean came in with several slices of pizza that Maggie shovelled down rapidly. She called Esme on Jean's mobile and, speaking in a low voice, told her that she was staying with a friend and would be back tomorrow morning. To her surprise, Esme sounded angry; she'd never been angry with her about anything.

'You can't just up and leave whenever the mood takes you, dearie. I had no idea where you'd gone. And what about your mum?'

And Maggie felt like shouting, 'What about her?' But she only said, 'Sorry.'

Esme lowered her own voice to a whisper then. 'I think I'll call the hospital tomorrow and tell them that she's here. It's the right thing to do. Don't you think? She seems a bit confused.'

Maggie said nothing to that. She didn't want to admit that she'd been hoping Esme would come to that conclusion. But only for her mum's sake, of course: Cynthia needed to be properly taken care of.

Maggie could hear the TV blaring in the background and she pictured her mum sitting in front of it, her face blank. Perhaps Hoagy was there too, lying with his chin upon her lap receiving lavish amounts of attention.

'I'll be back early tomorrow,' she said and abruptly ended the call.

Maybe it was because Esme didn't want to spend an awkward evening alone with Cynthia? Well, Maggie could understand that, but tough luck. And she felt vindicated. Esme thought her mother was unwell too; she wasn't just making it up.

When Maggie looked up, Jean was staring at her. 'Why do you have to hide me from your mum?' Maggie asked in a loud voice.

Jean put a finger to her lips. 'Ssssh, can't you?' she whispered. 'My mum doesn't really like me having friends over. Especially if she hasn't made sure that they're suitable first.'

'Suitable?'

Jean shrugged. 'She's convinced I'm going to fall in with the wrong crowd, get an awful boyfriend, get pregnant and addicted to drugs, pretty much all at the same time.' Jean shook her head. 'And she wants me to go to Oxford, because that's what she wished she could have done. Obviously, there's no way I'm going there, but I haven't told her that yet.'

'I'm not exactly a bad influence,' Maggie said, almost laughing.

'Do you get perfect grades? Are you top of the class?'

'Um, no, I'm more like the bottom.'

'Then she won't like you. And she's not going to be too crazy about the fact that there's a white crow following you round wherever you go. That could be a slight issue for her.'

They both burst out laughing and quickly covered their mouths. The bird had been serenely roosting in one of Jean's bookshelves and now it peered at Maggie quizzically, as if confused. Maggie was pretty sure it didn't have a great sense of humour.

'She wants me to be very, very normal and unbelievably high achieving at the same time,' Jean continued. 'And unluckily for her, I'm neither.'

Maggie sighed: no one's parents seemed to have a clue.

And so now here she was, lying in this dense, unfamiliar darkness. She didn't exactly wish she was back at Milton Lodge, but she kind of wished she wasn't here either.

After a while Jean whispered, 'Are you awake?'

'Yeah.'

'Are you OK?'

'Yeah.'

'You know, I'd love to have a crow following me around all day. Don't let it get you down. It's cool.'

It must have been the darkness that made it easier to talk. 'It's not a crow,' Maggie found herself saying.

'So it *is* a spirit,' Jean's voice was full of excitement, 'or a ghost?'

'I don't actually know,' Maggie said flatly. 'It hasn't bothered to tell me.'

'Still, it's a very chilled-out ghost, or whatever. It doesn't want much, does it?'

'It wants *everything*,' Maggie burst out.

'Really? I've never even seen it eat anything; it just sips water occasionally.'

'There are other things.'

'Like what?'

'Jean, you don't understand. It's . . .' Again, the darkness protected her from what she was going to say. 'It's from another place . . . it's from another world.'

Maggie could hear that Jean had bolted up in her bed. 'Are you actually serious?'

'Yeah. But I promise you, this bird can follow me round till the end of time. I won't go back there.'

'Woah.' Jean's voice was full of respect and awe. Maggie could see her white Nirvana T-shirt glowing in the darkness beside her. 'I *knew* stuff like that existed. I always did. Why don't you want to go back?'

'Because it's horrible. It's dark almost all the time. And it's full of awful people that want to hurt you. It's an unhappy place.'

There was a longer pause. 'Is that where you and Ida disappeared to? I mean, last term when there was all that fuss?'

'Yeah. Um, I had to go and get her.'

Jean blew air out of her mouth, 'Pfff, she's lucky someone cares enough to bother.'

'What do you mean?'

'Ida Beechwood is a cow. Or hadn't you noticed?'

Maggie's cheeks flushed in the darkness. 'She is not. She's my friend.'

'I bet she still bullies you, even though you're "friends".'

'She does not.'

'Whatever.'

'It's true. She's not really like that. I mean, she does boss me around a bit. But I've seen . . .' Maggie broke off. No one wanted to hear that she could read other people's emotions. It would scare even this girl.

'What have you seen?'

'Nothing. I just mean she's all right really. She's more insecure than you think.'

'Of course she's insecure,' Jean said definitively. 'That's obvious. But I've observed her and she's a classic bully. Avoid 'em at all costs. That's what I say.'

Maggie didn't bother replying. She sat up, her skin all hot from the synthetic material of the sleeping bag. She badly wanted to leave but she just didn't know how to say it, or how to make her limbs start moving.

'So Ida knows all about this other world too? It's so not fair she got to go.'

'She can't recall much of it. And honestly, she had an awful time there. She had bad dreams for a bit, but I think she's kind of forgotten it all now. She never talks about it.'

'This is so unbelievably cool, Maggie. I just knew there was something interesting about you. And that's the first time I've ever said that about a Fortlake pupil . . . all of them are so dull. Little over-privileged capitalists who just can't wait to be exactly like Mummy and Daddy. They all want the same two things: to be pretty and have the best clothes or phones.'

Maggie didn't think it was the right time to admit that these were amongst her main aspirations too. But Jean was soon back to her favourite new subject.

'Can you take me there, do you think? To this other world place?'

'No, no way. It's a nightmare.'

'I'd just love to have a look.'

'Forget it. And don't tell anyone what I said. I don't even know why I told you.'

'All right. Don't freak out.'

When she woke the next morning, Jean was still asleep and the flat was silent. She got dressed hurriedly and ran out of the flat, not caring if she bumped into Jean's grades-obsessed mother or not.

The heat was not up yet; it was still dormant in the sky above the clouds. The little crow bumped along content-edly in her bag, but looking at it reminded her of what she'd said to Jean last night. She felt a deep pang of regret and embarrassment. Telling people secrets was always a mistake – she couldn't seem to learn that simple rule. She always blurted something out. Now crazy Jean would think *she* was crazy. Perhaps she would tell someone . . .

She trudged back to Milton Lodge. When she got there, she found the back door wasn't closed. Inside, Hoagy was on the floor, tummy-side up, snoring like a trooper. His long curving scar stared up at her like an admonishment.

But the sofa where her mum had been sleeping was empty.

She went to check the bathroom but the door was wide open with no one inside, and the toilet was empty too. Maggie ran out into the garden, but apart from several fat wood pigeons who took off as she approached, it was deserted. Cynthia Brown had gone.

11

EVERYTHING HAS CHANGED

He watched them arrive, figures on the other side of the lake. The orbs hovered above them, illuminating everything. Oz climbed down to the forest floor, but let his arms stay wrapped around the vast tree trunk. He listened to the ancient tree breathing for several moments then set out towards the house.

It was very dark, the moon blocked by clouds, but Oz knew the way so well he could have done it with his eyes closed. He ran round the edge of the lake, his chest rasping with the cold, until he drew closer. Then he dipped into the shadows and watched.

The orbs hung over a cart that had clearly been dragged there by the four exhausted umons: sweat was steaming off them up into the chilly air. There was a body in the cart and it wasn't moving. Was it the girl? Had they killed her already?

But then the body sat up and it smiled. Though it was not a girl; it was a woman, thin and fragile looking with very short hair. She looked out across the lake, dull like dark steel, and breathed in deeply. Her eyes shone in the light cast by the orbs. She was happy to be in this awful place. She must be mad, Oz thought. And who was she?

At that moment, Almarra appeared. She raised one spindly finger and an orb rose into the sky. It drifted up until it was right above the unknown woman, then without warning it descended like a steeping hawk and struck her in the back of the neck. The woman cried out and slumped forward, unconscious. Oz managed to stifle his own cry of shock. But then something truly strange happened. . .

Eldrow came out of the house and went straight towards the cart. He shoved Almarra aside with such force that she would have fallen if one of the guards had not caught her. The orbs rose, ready to strike, but the sorcerer shook her head and stood watching – Oz could not make out her expression.

For a terrible moment he thought his father was going to attack the unconscious woman. But instead, he fell down beside the cart and began to sob. In the cold night air Oz listened to his father crying. He felt repelled by this sudden breakdown in someone who had no feelings – and it frightened him. It came into his mind that he must have fallen asleep in the trees; that this could not be real. But no amount of pinching his skin would make the scene go away.

Nobody moved until Eldrow had recovered himself. He picked the woman up in his arms and carried her into the house. Almarra and the orbs followed. Then the guards dragged the exhausted umons away and it was as if no one had ever been there. Oz was left with an empty stage and a mind racing to try and comprehend what had just unfolded.

He lay on his bed and waited until the house was very still; the sort of stillness that only comes when people are sleeping, breathing in that secret slow way. He knew the orbs liked to drift around the place, or run around the corridors as the nasty golden-eyed boys, but he couldn't hear anything. Besides, they hardly seemed to notice him any more. It was worth the risk.

He slipped out of his room and stood listening. Then he moved silently to the long passageway that connected the different parts of the house. Outside the sky had cleared and the moon hung serenely above the lake, almost full.

He crept along to his father's room. The door was ajar and a lamp burnt low. By its faint light he could see the empty unmade bed, bottles strewn everywhere, and piles of ancient books. It smelt musty and unclean, but there was no sign of Eldrow.

The upper rooms were Almarra's domain: if his father had gone up there with the unknown woman, he'd have to give up. But there was one other possibility: a small door in the hallway that was never used. He had wondered about it for some time, but had never dared to investigate. Now, his heart beating hard, he approached it as silently as a little cat and pushed gently at the dark wood.

To his surprise, it swung open and revealed a flight of stone steps that led down to an underground floor. There were a few lanterns spitting and sputtering on the walls, enough to see by. Oz took a deep breath and descended. It was quite steep and at the bottom it felt cold and damp. There was a narrow corridor that looked as if it ran the full width of the house. He didn't like it, he was afraid, but somehow it was impossible to turn around and go back to bed . . .

After a short walk, he came to a turn that led in the direction of the lake. There were lanterns here too, brighter ones, the smell of fresh peat burning within them cloying and intense. Oz hesitated; he could not see where the passage ended. But now he could hear a very quiet murmuring voice, drifting up to him in the silence. He forced himself to keep moving forwards and down.

At the end of the passageway there were dark empty cells on both sides, except for one on the right that glowed with light. And now he recognised the voice as his father's. It sounded as if he was trying to soothe or sing someone to sleep. All was silent but for this voice. It ebbed and flowed, like water moving. It was hypnotic and Oz was drawn to it and drawn to the warm light. He edged towards the cell and peered inside.

The short-haired woman he had seen in the cart was now

lying on a narrow bed. She was sleeping or unconscious under a heavy white blanket. But her face still radiated peace and contentment. The orb hovering above her, bathed her in a deep golden light that seemed unusually benign.

The shifter sensed Oz's presence, but it tolerated him. Oz had heard tales of how the orbs could get into your head, read your deepest, darkest thoughts, and even control you. But he had been spared that so far, perhaps because he was Eldrow's son. Or perhaps it was simply because they already knew what they would find . . . that he was lonely and a coward. That he was afraid of and hated Almarra. These were hardly big secrets.

Eldrow was kneeling beside the woman. Oz had never seen him so calm, and he was singing the sweet song over and over again.

After a while, Oz dared to speak. 'Who is this?'

The lullaby broke off and Eldrow turned to him, but showed no surprise at his presence. After a long pause, he said, 'She is here to lure Maggie Blue back to the Island.'

'And you know her?'

'She is Maggie Blue's mother.' He turned back to the woman and tenderly took her limp hand.

What Oz noticed were Eldrow's eyes, his huge grey eyes: they had softened, no longer cold and inhuman. His father had never looked at *him* that way. So why had he taken him away from the one person who did love him? Oz hated this creepy house, the soulless hideout of the soulless Almarra.

And he wished he had never seen the Fathers and the horrifying beings that lurked in their dark pool, and now in his dreams. He would rather have stayed with Suri and taken his chances in Sun City.

He looked enviously at the serene woman bathed in light. Oz wished he could climb under the heavy snow-white blanket and lie beside her. But now his father beckoned him very close. He pressed his mouth to Oz's ear so that the orb would not hear.

'Listen, boy,' he whispered urgently, 'everything has changed: for me, and so for you too. From now on, just do what I tell you. Don't ask any questions. You obey *me*; you listen to *me*. Nothing else matters . . . *nothing else matters*. Do you understand?'

Oz did not. And though he didn't have a single rebellious bone in his body, he also did not understand why he should obey this man, this stranger who cared nothing for him. But while he was considering this radical idea, he had to keep up appearances. So he only nodded.

'Good.'

'But . . . ?'

'I said, don't ask questions.'

'But what should I do now?' Oz whispered.

'Get out of my sight.'

Oz didn't need to be asked twice. He fled back along the underground corridor, up the steep stairs and back to his empty room.

12

THE OWL, THE GIRL
AND THE PUSSYCAT

Any eager twitchers in the West Minchen area would have been interested to observe the monstrous grey owl and the equally enormous jet-black crow sitting glumly side by side at the bottom of Milton Lodge's garden. Both were far larger than any ever seen before and would have caused a sensation. But the two birds were unaware of this and sat with their fierce and beady eyes, respectively, fixed upon the windows of the girl's house.

They were both exhausted: Duma had been on the tail of Maggie and the white crow since last night, and had spent all night perched uncomfortably on a lamppost – the only place from which he could clearly keep an eye on the back window of the flat the girl had disappeared into. Well, not quite the only perch. Initially he'd found a very serviceable spot on a nearby balcony, but an old lady had shooed him away with a copy of the *Radio Times* and a bucket of water.

He had not anticipated the girl would stay away all night. And he was bad-tempered on his return, especially when he learnt that Ulrich had more significant things to report.

Ulrich had not slept either. He had seen the woman being taken in the early hours. He had watched, utterly focused and calm now that things were finally happening, as two orbs appeared in the sky and drifted casually down into the garden, hovering ominously by the ground-floor windows. They gave a low whistle and almost at once, three shifters (some of the mercenary shifters Ulrich often saw, and whom he knew had been observing the girl for as long as he had) crept around the side of the house: a snouter and two large cats. Ulrich guessed they were coming to kidnap Maggie and would be shocked to find that for once the girl wasn't there.

The snouter, a small lithe creature with a russet back, white belly and long pink nose, had shimmied up a pipe attached to the wall. From the top of this it managed to cling onto the frame of a small upper window, open a crack for air. Its sinewy body had then slipped inside and moments later, a small red-haired man had opened the back door and the others had entered.

But to Ulrich's surprise, they quickly appeared again, and they were carrying Maggie's mother. Her wrists had been tied in front of her and her feet were bound too. But Ulrich heard no sounds of any sort of resistance. He assumed that the woman had been given something to calm her. Or perhaps the orbs had dealt with her in their usual violent way. Whatever had occurred, the orbs now glided behind the little party who moved briskly away into the darkness.

Ulrich waited until they had disappeared down the side of the house into the darkness before rising up into the air. He climbed to a high enough altitude that they would be unlikely to sense him. With his huge eyes he could view them perfectly, even in darkness – not that there was ever any real darkness here. Besides, he knew where they were going.

He followed them calmly as they ran the familiar route. A few of the extraordinary lighted vehicles that so dominated this world eased past them at speed, but none of the inhabitants seemed to take any notice, or if they did, they were untroubled by what they saw – a defenceless person being carried away in the night. And so the curious cabal moved unhindered towards the woods.

As they disappeared through the gate and under the canopy, Ulrich flew over the tops of the trees until he was at about the right spot, then he darted down through the branches. He was just in time to see all of them disappear through the portal. He hesitated, wondering whether to follow them. But he thought better of it and flew back slowly to his perch to wait. It was the girl's mother after all, and Roda had never given any orders concerning her.

The girl herself returned, somewhat dishevelled, in the early morning, followed by an equally dishevelled and grumpy Duma. She found her mother missing and raised the alarm. She and the older lady had talked for some time and then set out to search the area. The two birds had diligently trailed them and were subsequently fairly exhausted and depressed.

'Why have they even taken this woman?' Duma asked grumpily.

'It seems they are using her as bait. And we will use her too.'

'How?'

'She is Maggie's mother.' He refrained from adding, *you idiot.*

'But won't she want to find this woman before she does anything for us?' Duma asked, his voice weary.

'Once she is through the portal, what she wants will have very little bearing on what happens,' Ulrich replied coldly. 'Now cross and find Roda. Tell him what is happening. I await his orders.'

With great relief, the owl watched as the sulky black bird heaved himself up into the sky and disappeared.

Night had fallen by the time Ulrich saw Maggie and the one-eyed cat again. On the girl's shoulder, like a mirage, an impossible miracle, the white crow sat placid and silent.

They disappeared round the side of the house and Ulrich swept silently up into the air.

He followed them down the main road and halfway down a smaller street. Behind him, he heard a familiar screeching. A great blue-grey heron was suddenly at his side, flying beside him: Roda, his master. Below them, Ulrich saw that a dark figure had stepped out of the shadows, and was also moving swiftly towards the girl.

She was blocking Maggie's path. There wasn't really anywhere to hide and instead Maggie felt the familiar red bubbling up inside her. But for the first time in many months, she didn't try and stop it – she let it flow.

'What?'

Ida's face emerged in the orange glow of a streetlight.

'The crow's still with you?'

'Looks like it.'

Ida glanced down at Hoagy who stood protectively by Maggie's legs. 'I came round earlier, because I wanted to . . .' She broke off.

'I saw you,' Maggie said. 'But it wasn't a good time. I didn't realise you would be waiting outside my house all this time else I would have brought you a cup of tea.'

'What's up with you? Why are you so angry?'

'Oh, and that *was* my mum on the sofa, in case you were wondering, the one that looked like a tramp, the one you turned your nose up at. And now she's gone missing, so don't worry, she won't bother you. Hoagy and me are looking for her.'

Maggie barely knew where it was coming from, this anger, but it just poured out. 'And yes, the white crow is definitely not normal and probably comes from the Dark World. Remember that place? The place you seem to have forgotten. The one I can't forget. But, seriously, don't worry about it. You just carry on being perfect. I'll deal with it.'

Ida's face crumpled slightly. For a moment Maggie thought she was going to cry. 'I haven't forgotten. I just wanted to see you . . . I need to tell you something . . .' Ida began. 'Wait, your mum's gone missing?'

Maggie nodded and suddenly all the adrenaline drained away and she felt tired and a bit afraid. 'She said someone was coming to get her and I told her she was crazy.' Shame pulsed quickly around Maggie's body. It turned out she was exactly like the people she thought she hated.

On the other side of the road, a woman walking her dog allowed it to root around by a tree so that she could get a good look at the white bird on Maggie's shoulder. But her little fluffy pooch strained at the lead when it saw Hoagy. In response, the old cat arched his back and hissed and spat violently and the dog started to howl with excitement. The woman pulled it back and walked quickly away.

'Thank goodness they keep those stupid mutts on leads,' Hoagy murmured and began to lick one of his front paws.

'Let me help you look for her,' Ida said quickly.

'We're not going to find her anyway,' Maggie said, suddenly sure that that was true.

She walked down the street, and Ida and the cat followed her. There was a faint hum of traffic behind them, but it was always so quiet and still round here after dark. The huge old houses on either side looked welcoming and cosy with their warm yellow interiors and TVs flickering against the deep-blue night. If she lived in one of these beautiful places, Maggie was sure that somehow her life would be beautiful too, and that she would feel complete.

Above them, they heard an owl hooting. Hoagy stopped and sniffed the air. 'An owl's fighting call,' he purred. 'It's not the right time of year for that . . .' His tattered-up ears swivelled around.

He listened a bit longer then shook his round head in confusion. 'Owls fight to the death over territory. If you find an injured one, never take it away from where it's been fighting. It will only die of a broken heart.'

'Fascinating,' Maggie said, not bothering to offer any explanation when Ida, who had only heard a series of expressive but indistinct purrs and mewls, looked at her in confusion. Let her feel lost for once, Maggie thought to herself.

As they neared the end of the street, Maggie noticed more and more neighbourhood cats peering out of front gates and sitting on garden walls watching their odd little procession. Some nodded or meowed to Hoagy who walked proudly along in the middle of the road. It seemed they were paying their feline respects to him.

'I must say this elder statesman role suits me down to the ground, don't you think, girlie?' he purred at her.

As if his head needed to expand any further, Maggie thought.

The hooting came right above them again, louder than ever, and Hoagy stopped and sniffed the air once more. Suddenly the white crow began to squawk loudly, making Maggie jump. It flew off her shoulder and fluttered up into the air, but it didn't seem afraid . . . it seemed more, well it was odd, but it seemed excited, almost happy. Maggie could feel it.

Then something fell out of the sycamore tree that stood on the corner. It touched Maggie's head lightly. She screamed and the thing flew away. She and Ida crouched down low against someone's garden wall, whilst Hoagy leapt up onto it and scanned the air, his whiskers twitching feverishly.

'It came right at you,' Ida said. She giggled nervously. 'What is it with you and birds, Maggie?'

'Oh, shut up!' Maggie snapped. She could feel Ida's shock at her anger, and it pleased her. She could hear the heavy beating of wings in the air and the crazed hootings getting closer. But then everything became eerily quiet again. She scanned the sky above them, but saw nothing.

Ida was looking at her. 'I do remember, but I don't want

to, OK? I know you saved me . . . I mean, I think about it every day. But it's traumatic. And I thought that bird was weird . . . you're . . . you're just impossible to talk to. It's like you don't want me to say anything.'

Maggie was more interested in this, but she felt the danger was near so she had to shush her friend again. She could sense something else there. She turned round and a few feet behind her she saw a grey owl in the middle of the road. It was motionless, just sitting there. She'd never seen one so huge. As she watched, it raised its wings high in an almost human gesture, like a greeting. Then it pressed its wings tight into its body, tucked its face down into its feathered breast and shifted.

Beside her, Ida screamed in shock because now there was a very large man standing in the bird's place, a man with gnarled hands and a long deep scar on one cheek. He stepped forward a little and looked at them exactingly with his huge yellow eyes. She became aware that the white crow was still in the air and was now flying in circles, cawing softly. She felt its happiness again. But why was it happy?

In the distance, from the direction of the high street, Maggie heard drunken shouts. She wished the drunks would walk up this way and disturb the scene, break it up in some way. But the voices faded and the night regained its hold. Only a plane somewhere high above them made its descending sigh into the darkness.

She felt Hoagy's fur against her legs.

'Maggie,' he hissed sharply, 'look!'

Maggie turned to look back the other way and she saw a heron perched upon an old brick wall that didn't look like it could take its weight. It was enormous, bigger than she remembered it in the moon witches' hut. And in her mind's eye, she saw its shadow falling out of the sky like an arrow, knocking Eldrow to the ground. The heron had saved her life, and yet the sight of it, its quivering feathers, made her feel uneasy. She realised she was trembling.

When it spoke, its voice was very clear: 'You must return.'

Maggie just kept staring at it: the great wings, the long snake-like neck and the cool beady eyes watching her.

The crow landed in the road beside her and its pure white body glowed soft and organic in the artificial light. What if someone passed by now? What if they pulled open their curtains to see what all the noise was about? Or to look at the moon which, Maggie now noticed, hung low in the sky at the end of the street.

She began to feel the soft mist descend into her mind. It was not like the orbs; it was gentle, considerate, but it was the same deal, wasn't it? The heron wanted to read her or direct her thoughts, or both. So she fought back. She wasn't sure how she was doing it, but she began to understand that she could keep him at bay. And it was the same with the other greener mist that came from the owl-man. She pushed it away. It was just like with the orbs – they could not control her. She smiled for a moment, enjoying this power. They could not make her do anything.

Hoagy stayed very close to Maggie's legs, watching. He could sense invisible particles moving in the air all around him, a strong energy that he did not understand. He remembered Dot's words when she learnt that Maggie had crossed through the portal alone: *not entirely human*. Who was Maggie Blue really? He still wasn't sure that he knew. And at that moment he didn't want to be with his beloved friend. Was it wrong that he longed to be with Esme, stretched out on her bed all safe and warm? His long scar ached, reminding him not to get into too much trouble.

Maggie had told him before that all bird shifters could be trusted. Hmmm, of course it sounded good on paper, but Hoagy had never been a huge fan. *Darn birds!*, he hissed through his sharp teeth.

What he also remembered, all too humiliatingly well, was this same ridiculously enormous heron swooping upon him in the Dark World and lifting him into the air in its talons. He didn't fancy another unchartered flight, especially on his stomping ground. The shame would be too hard to live down even with his newly sanctified ancient cat status. Although currently out of sight, he knew that all the local felines were watching and that this night theatre would be the talk of the mog community for many days to come.

To his great relief, Maggie didn't even deign to respond to these avian brutes. She turned abruptly on her heels and began walking very quickly back towards the main road and Milton Lodge. He and Ida scrambled after her. And for a moment they seemed happy to let them go. Only the white crow flew above Maggie, refusing to be parted from her.

But they had only got about halfway up the street, Maggie marching determinedly ahead, when the cat heard rapid footsteps behind them. He turned and saw the owl-man running towards them at a frightening speed. Maggie had only just turned when, in one flowing movement, the huge man knocked her off her feet and grabbed her with one of his gnarled hands. She screamed and started kicking and scrabbling, but his powerful arm only tightened around her.

Behind him, its huge wingspan grazing the parked cars as it took off, the great heron kept low to the ground. The owl-man, still carrying his kicking and screaming cargo, had already reached the main road. There were no cars coming and enough space for the heron to fly right beside him as he ran. With his huge arms, the owl-man hoisted Maggie onto the heron's back and the great bird swept high into the sky. Beside him, Ida screamed and began to run wildly up the street. And Hoagy followed.

In the middle of the deserted road, they watched as the owl-man wrapped his arms around his body and tucked his great head into his chest. And suddenly he too was flying: a magnificent grey owl propelling itself into the night sky. And inevitably, cawing loudly, the white crow flew after them. Then they were all gone; Maggie's screams faded away, Ida ran round the corner as fast as she could.

The cat was left alone, completely stunned in the silent street.

13

AGAIN

Maggie was no longer fighting; she was holding on for dear life. The heron's feathers were greasy, and she was terrified that she might slip off at any moment. Beside them, the owl and the white crow kept pace and Maggie did not need to be told where they were going. The familiar streets flashed past below them, the electric glow of house windows and moving cars.

And then they were over the dark undulating mass where no lights shone. It looked like a black ocean. Somewhere near the middle, the heron dived down into the trees, and Maggie ducked her head to avoid the snapping and falling branches. They were making for the portal.

Maggie tried to get her bearings but everything was so dark and confusing. The bird would have to get very low to the ground, she thought, to pass through the portal without stopping. She would roll off at the last second, so it would go through and she'd be left behind. She couldn't see anything, and branches kept snapping at her face.

'I will not go back,' Maggie hissed deep into the heron's oily feathers, '*I will not!*'. As if sensing her plan, it lifted its great wings and rolled them over her, so that the softer inner feathers were on the outside.

Maggie was screaming it now, 'I will not, I will nooooooo...'

They descended so fast they nearly hit the ground and the heron had to jerk up. He steadied himself . . . and then they collided with something solid. The heron screeched and dropped, slightly stunned, to the forest floor. The two other birds crashed down beside him a few seconds later. Maggie fell off the heron's back and despite her head spinning, she got to her feet at once and started running. But she'd only managed to get a few feet away before thick strong hands grabbed her and wrestled her to the ground.

She spat out the leaves and soil from her mouth and lay there panting for a while, exhausted. When she turned over and looked up, she saw the white crow above her. It was perching in a tree branch and light came off it in a soft glow. It was peaceful and Maggie closed her eyes.

When she opened them again, she saw the heron and the owl-man beside her. The heron was impassive, but looking more closely at the owl-man, Maggie thought that his face was not unkind, even if his body wasn't suited to anything other than brute force.

Then something occurred to her. 'Did I stop us crossing?'

'Yes,' the heron replied. It was staring at her with an intense but unreadable expression.

'I'm not going back,' Maggie said.

'You are.'

The heron looked up briefly into the sky then back at Maggie. 'We have been looking after you for long enough.'

'Looking after me?' Maggie said. 'No one's been looking after me.'

Ulrich rolled his enormous eyes. 'Oh really.'

'Really.' Maggie's eyes flashed.

'Then what have I been doing sitting in an oak tree losing my mind with boredom for the past seven moons?'

'I've got no idea. I didn't ask for your help,' Maggie retorted.

'But you should be thankful for it all the same,' said the heron. 'My name is Roda,' he nodded at the owl, 'this is Ulrich. And you must believe us when we tell you that you are in danger. And that we are not the only ones who have been watching you. There are others too.'

Maggie felt panic rising. She thought she'd got away but perhaps the Dark World had never left her alone; it had all been an illusion. She felt heavy and low. Her anger, her outrage, was draining away.

'Don't you care about your mother?' the heron asked.

'What about her?'

'Shifters have taken her,' the owl-man said. 'I watched them do it.'

Maggie turned her attention to him once more.

'They bound her hands and feet,' he went on. 'She is very frail – I'm not sure she will survive it.'

'Why should I believe what you're saying?'

'Because it's true,' the heron replied. 'And you feel it.'

Maggie said nothing; she didn't argue. In her heart, she did feel that no amount of looking in this world would uncover Cynthia Brown.

'Why would they take *her*? She's got nothing to do with anything.'

'But you won't leave your mother to suffer, will you?'

'But why does anyone care about me? Why can't you all just leave me alone?'

'Everyone is interested in your connection to the Great O.'

Maggie's anger surged back reassuringly. 'I wouldn't know this Great O thing if I bumped into it on the street, OK? I came to your world to rescue my friend, *once*, and I am never going back.'

'Then our world will die.'

'Why should I care? It's a horrible world and I hope it does die.' She enjoyed the shock on their faces when she said it. But her triumph was fleeting. She felt trapped.

Why couldn't her mum have stayed where she was in the hospital? Why did she have to come here? If Cynthia was in the Dark World, what hope did she have without Maggie? Anger and fear pulsed round her until she thought she might burst. They knew they had her, that she was powerless after all. She wanted to scream. But she couldn't. Everything had to be bottled up inside, else she wouldn't be able to carry on and face it. She had to be strong.

Maggie stayed still for a very long time. In the sky above her, the white crow still cast its faint but comforting light. At least it would be with her.

'If I cross, I won't do anything to help you.'

Roda nodded gravely. He moved towards the arched old tree, but Maggie rushed forward and pushed the bird aside.

'*I* will do it.'

Suddenly there was a crashing noise from amidst the trees and the sound of gasping and sobbing. Maggie looked round and saw Ida there. She looked dishevelled and slightly wild.

'Maggie!' she cried out. 'Please, don't. Please don't go back there.'

'I have to.'

'Please . . . !' Ida sounded hysterical. 'Listen to me!'

But Maggie turned away and stepped towards the arching gnarled tree. And suddenly and very easily she could see it once again – the window into another world. The white crow flew down to her shoulder still emanating the wonderful soft light, and Maggie let her mind go blank.

She had to admit, it gave her pleasure to feel the tingle in her fingers, as she peeled back the layers between the worlds. Then her whole body began to shake with the electricity, with the power. There before her was the familiar dark forest, the same but so frighteningly different. And yet, for a moment, its darkness comforted her too.

Just as she threw herself in, she heard Ida give a blood-curdling scream behind her. She tried to turn round, but it was too late. The crow fell into her arms and holding onto its soft fragile body, Maggie vanished into the other world.

PART TWO

14

NEW ENSEMBLE

A fly was buzzing around the room, building to a fever pitch of desperation as it dashed itself against the glass. By all the cats, they were stupid. Even the dumbest mog in the world could locate an open window and get out of it. Hoagy lay on the sofa, following the fly's erratic movements around with his one eye. He was in a terrible mood.

Last night . . . he kept replaying it in his mind: the owl-man, as big as an oak, grabbing Maggie in his huge hands and running off with her as if she weighed nothing; the great blue-grey heron, rising slowly into the orange night. He knew where they were taking her, of course. The girl, Ida, had run after them. Pah! What did she think *she* could do?

Hoagy remembered when they had found Ida in the Dark World: her body all crumpled up in the huge glass container, her skin yellowish, her school uniform a sack around her body. She had been a sleeper, though not for long. She was better off than the others. Maggie had told him that Ida couldn't remember anything, or at least not much.

Hoagy did not like her. Was he a little jealous? he wondered, daring himself to be honest. It was true, he had grown foolishly fond of Maggie Blue, and all felines knew that fondness for the legendarily unreliable humans was never a good shout. But no, it wasn't quite like that. It was more that this other girl seemed to subdue Maggie; she made her quiet and obedient; that is, unlike herself. And Hoagy found that very odd – he didn't understand why this far more conventional girl had so much power over his beloved friend.

In fact, last night was the first time he'd ever seen Maggie tell Ida to shut up. And, yes, this had pleased the old cat greatly. But what did any of that matter now? For the first time in his long feline life, he felt completely helpless. He had to face it: he was too old and decrepit to help his dearest friend.

The fly was now throwing itself against the mirror, trying to knock itself out. Hoagy gritted his teeth – if it didn't succeed in its task soon, he would gladly lend a paw. His sharp claws appeared and then slowly retracted, warming up for a possible run-in.

But then, two things happened: Esme appeared, stumbling out of her room, bleary eyed as usual, make-up smudged on her face. And at the same moment, a very tall girl in a purple jumpsuit knocked on the back door.

Esme hurried over, wrapping her dressing gown around her and trying, unsuccessfully, to improve her bird's-nest hair as she went. She opened the door. 'Yes?'

The tall girl looked at her carefully. 'Is this where Maggie Blue lives?'

'Yes. Who are you?'

'Oh, I'm Jean. A friend of hers . . . well, actually I've only known her a day or two.' Esme only stared at her, so after a pause she continued. 'She stayed over at my house the other night, and you were annoyed about it?'

'Oh right, yes. Well, come in, come in.'

'Is Maggie here?' Jean asked, peering into the dim room. Hoagy noticed how she took everything in with alert curiosity.

'Um, she should be,' muttered Esme who was looking at the sofa where Maggie slept, taking in the lack of shoes and the pile of music still on one side of it from the night before. 'Oh my God, where is she?'

She rushed to check the bathroom and then pushed past Jean into the garden. After a few minutes she reappeared and slumped onto the sofa. She put her head in her hands.

Jean looked panicked. 'I'm sure she's fine. She's probably gone out for a walk or something.'

Esme shook her head. There was a horribly awkward pause when even the deranged fly remained respectfully silent. Jean was looking over at Hoagy, as if hoping he would intervene. She seemed unusually aware that he was real.

Hoagy tried talking to her. 'Can you hear me?'

The girl smiled, came over to him and started scratching him behind the ear, which was delightful.

'Can you hear me?' he tried again. But clearly she could not.

Maggie's mum had been the same – more aware than the average human (though that wasn't saying much). He had taken to Cynthia rather a lot. Beneath all the layers, he was drawn to the person inside . . . she wasn't too unlike Maggie when it came down to it. A bit less angry perhaps. Or else the anger had been pushed somewhere deeper.

Esme was still hunched over, her hands covering her face, a crumpled bedraggled figure.

'Maggie was saying some, well, pretty crazy stuff,' Jean began. 'I mean, when she stayed over at mine. I totally believe her and everything, but it was a bit wild.'

Esme looked over at her, and her voice was unexpectedly sharp. 'What did she tell you?'

'Well . . .' the girl scratched her head and tilted it to one side, 'it's kind of difficult to know where to start . . .'

'Just tell me.'

Jean shrugged. 'First of all, there was this white crow that was following her around. It wasn't normal; it wasn't like a bird, really, if that makes any sense?'

It was clear from Esme's face that it didn't.

'Then she said that when she disappeared last year, she went to another world through this hole she found in the woods. It's dark and horrible there, apparently. Um, oh yeah, then Miss Cane from school was actually a wolf and she kidnapped Ida and took her to this other world. And Maggie rescued her and brought her back.' She broke off, somewhat helplessly. 'That's the short version.'

Hoagy's fur bristled . . . it seemed he had been air-brushed out of events.

But Jean suddenly looked over at him and said, 'Oh, and this cat went with her and helped her, and, er, it can talk apparently. Maggie talks to the cat. It all sounds pretty stupid when I'm saying it out loud to you. Ha!' She smiled and pulled a face.

But Esme wasn't smiling. 'You're saying the cat can talk?'

'Maggie said.'

Esme shook her head. 'But that is crazy.'

Hoagy's tail flickered angrily from side to side. The narrowness of the human mind never failed to irritate and, frankly, deeply offend him. And at this moment it was more the latter. They could never see beyond the end of their own unrefined snouts. Pah!

Esme's face creased with worry. 'Maybe she has the same problems as her mother?'

'Or maybe you're just an idiot,' Hoagy hissed.

Esme looked at him strangely then shook her head. 'I'm not going to mess around this time. I'm calling the police. Maggie and her mum are both missing now. This has got to stop.'

Hoagy began mewling very loudly. 'Don't. Don't, you idiot.'

Esme looked down at him in astonishment. 'What are you making such a racket about?'

She stroked him absently on the head. But Hoagy kept at it, whining and complaining. And when Esme stood up to get to the phone, Hoagy rushed round and round her legs, hissing.

Esme nearly tripped over him. 'What's going on, puss?'

The old cat ran nimbly ahead and jumped up onto the little telephone table so that it wobbled violently with the hefty impact. And as Esme approached, he put his body over the phone receiver.

'Do get off, my love,' Esme said gently. 'Come on.'

But as she reached for the phone, the old cat hissed violently and bared his teeth. Esme drew back in astonishment.

The girl in purple had watched his performance with interest. She said quietly, 'I think he's trying to tell you something.'

Hoagy immediately started purring as loudly as he could. Esme stared at him, then looked back at Jean, then back at him again.

The cat took this as his cue and did a rather alarming

thumping flop off the phone table and ran, tail high, back into the living room. Calling the police would just waste an awful lot of time. He looked around desperately. Then he remembered the one souvenir Maggie had kept from their strange adventure.

He rushed over to the small chest of drawers that Esme had cleared out so Maggie had somewhere to put her stuff. He nudged the lower drawer with his head and started mewling loudly. Esme, frowning in disbelief, came over and opened it, still looking at him in astonishment. He had to admit, it was really rather gratifying to be considered a sentient being for once, instead of a dumb beast. If only he could deliver his lecture on Billy Crystal's finest performances of the eighties and early nineties, she'd be spitting chips! One step at a time.

He got up on his hind legs and started pushing things around, but it was all just clothes. Hmmm. He leapt up onto the chest of drawers, scattering Maggie's clutter, and tapped at the smaller top drawer with his paw. Esme obliged once again but there seemed to be nothing there but a few books, pencils, hair bands and cheap bracelets.

But then she spied it. Esme reached into the very back and brought out a small wooden box.

'What's that?' Jean asked, jostling up next to Esme and reaching out as if she would take it.

But Esme was already opening it. And something dropped out, a small roll of paper. It was the parchment

Dot had given them and that Maggie had innocently presented to the ancient moon witch who had wanted to kill them.

Hoagy began to purr wildly and Esme reached out and stroked his solid old head. 'My clever puss.'

Hoagy raised his eyebrow – still patronising then. But as Esme opened the note his purr dried up. In his desperation, he hadn't really thought it through: the note was indecipherable, made up of the strange moon-witch hieroglyphics, or whatever they were. It was strange, certainly, but no indicator of where Maggie had gone or the kind of trouble she was in.

'What is that stuff?' Jean asked, fascinated, peering in as close as Esme would allow her.

'It's Dot's writing, I think,' Esme was saying, her voice catching a little. She shook her head. 'I knew she was caught up in all of this somehow.'

After staring at the tiny symbols for a little longer, Esme announced, 'I've seen this script before.'

It was Hoagy's turn to be astonished: his one eye popped wide open and he positively stared at her.

'You have?' Jean exclaimed.

Excitement rattled in the air.

Esme nodded. 'And I know just who to show it to.'

15

THE CHASE

When Maggie opened her eyes she could only see darkness. But she could hear noise all around: awful shrieks, cries and the thud of bodies coming together. The white crow quivered in her grasp and disappeared into her pocket. Then something struck her in the face – something hard and soft at the same time – and she fell back, screaming, into wet cold leaves.

Recovering, Maggie dragged herself over to the gnarled ancient tree and gripped it tightly, curling her body up protectively. Gradually her eyes adjusted as the noise above and around her intensified. She began to see wings and bodies silhouetted against the sky, just for an instant, and dark shapes writhing and moving in front of her. Then a new source of light flooded the scene: Maggie cowered down as four orbs appeared overhead, and what they illuminated was an awful sight.

The forest floor was a rippling sea of animals, some

strange, some familiar: badgers, stoats, purple rats, enormous cats with glowing eyes, wolves . . . and they were fighting against an endless flow of birds that dropped on them from the sky and the trees, descending at speed towards them with their beaks and claws poised to rip at their flesh and peck at their eyes. Most often the birds would manage to strike, draw blood, and then fly up again. But sometimes they would be dragged to earth and blood and feathers would mingle amid wild screeching and wailing.

As the battle raged, the orbs hovered around watching calmly, occasionally striking a bird as it descended, sending it tumbling off to the ground in pain to be pounced upon by others. They seemed to be looking for something.

Maggie had not noticed Ulrich and Roda arrive through the portal, but now she saw the heron drop down like a dark arrow, and close by, the owl was battering a long-bodied blue-ish animal against a tree. Maggie fought the urge to be sick. Whatever plan she had to rescue her mum, the only thing to do now was to cross back to West Minchen and wait for this hideous violence to end.

The white crow nestled deeper into her pocket and she felt its warmth – yes, she must make a move and quickly. But when she looked properly, she realised she was not by the portal, as she'd imagined, but a few feet away. In the short distance between the two trees, bodies writhed, locked in violence. Right beside her, a reddish weasel suddenly flung itself into the air and grabbed a sparrow that was attempting to get away. The two creatures rolled in the dust, the bird pecking manically at its opponent, the weasel clawing back as wildly.

Maggie pushed herself right down into the leaves so that she was on her stomach and crawled away from the fighting. She got about twenty feet into the darkness before she turned to her left and went along until she judged herself about parallel with the portal. She waited a few moments to make sure no one was watching her, then began moving slowly towards it.

A brown wolf whose face was already grizzled with blood and a hawk of some kind rolled into her path. Maggie froze and waited, hardly daring to breathe, as the wolf tried to pin the hawk down. But somehow the bird slipped away and, giving a tremendous shriek, propelled itself back into the dark air.

Maggie pressed her head into the leaves and took a few deep breaths. Then she wriggled as fast as she could towards the portal. But just as she was about to reach it, a bright light stunned her. Blinking hard, she made out an orb hovering right in front of her. 'No!' Maggie put her hands out to protect herself. But instead of the inevitable searing pain, something else hit her so that she fell to her side and onto a soft but solid surface that appeared to be moving fast.

The owl was flying through the trees at an alarming speed and she gripped onto his grey feathers for dear life. 'Ulrich!'

She closed her eyes, feeling his powerful sinews swerve beneath her. Suddenly he pitched up sharply and a few seconds later, branches snapping wickedly across her face and hands, they burst out into the freezing air.

They had cleared the trees and Maggie cried out, hoarse with relief, 'You saved me!'

'You do need looking after then,' the owl shrieked back.

The wind at this altitude was loud and very cold, so they said nothing more. A haze of purple light glimmered on the distant horizon but otherwise all was peacefully dark and the sounds of fierce fighting quickly faded away. Maggie submerged herself as deeply as she could within the owl's warm feathers and hung on tightly.

Below her was only darkness and she began to imagine that they were flying over water. She recalled the black choppy waters she had seen crashing against the coast below Almarra's tower. What if she fell off? What if she smashed down into the suffocating black waves? What if really it was the owl's mission to kill her? To drown her in the deep water where no one would ever find her? She was suddenly gripped with fear and her heart began pounding.

The little crow's sleek head appeared and snuggled into Maggie's chest trying to comfort her. For reasons unknown, this resilient little bird wanted to protect her and would not leave her. She felt that. There had never been anyone quite like that . . . Well, Hoagy had proved himself, hadn't he? Still, this connection was somehow different to his precious steadfast friendship. It was beyond choice . . .

Suddenly Ulrich's head snapped back and his wild yellow eyes stared past her. Maggie, too, began to feel something in the freezing particles around her. She dared a quick look back and saw them – distant still, but distinct, like four dog-stars hurtling towards them. Orbs. Above her, the crazed clusters of stars seemed to quiver in fear.

'Hold on!' the owl screeched.

And with no further warning he plummeted down. Maggie hung on for dear life. She couldn't see anything and she screamed as they fell. They were going to hit the ground, but at the last moment the owl swerved up and Maggie saw that they were flying low over the forest floor, the trunks coming at them from every angle.

She didn't dare look round again for fear of falling off. The owl kept up the mad speed, flying for what felt like forever. Until, at last, he crash-landed into a tree with a huge hollow in its ancient trunk. They clattered into the space and Maggie bashed her head painfully. But as she cried out, the owl's wings smothered the sound at once.

She could feel his heart going ten to the dozen, reverberating through her own body. It was a squash in there and the air quickly became hot and claustrophobic. Maggie tried to get more comfortable but Ulrich held her tight. 'Don't move.'

She stayed obediently motionless for some time. And

then between the owl's feathers she saw the orbs appear through the trees. They hovered together a little way away, aware of them, but still unsure. Maggie felt like her breath was making a deafening sound in the silence.

As the glowing balls of light hummed towards them, a sense of dread rose up inside Maggie: they were trapped.

'It's no good,' whispered Ulrich. 'We have to move. Are you ready?'

Maggie didn't have time to answer. She felt a sharp push and, screaming, she fell out of the tree and onto the soft damp ground. Ulrich was immediately beside her, but the orbs swarmed and only a blow from one of his great wings could keep them momentarily at bay.

Maggie threw herself onto the owl's back and he laboriously rose up towards the canopy, his breath ragged from exhaustion. But the orbs were all over them, slamming into the great bird's body so that he convulsed in pain. In desperation, the owl made a sudden backward punch with his right wing. As he did, his body swivelled violently and Maggie couldn't hold on any longer. She fell to the ground and landed with a painful thump. A sharp pain ran down her spine and she screamed, her face twisting in agony. She wondered if she could still move. A loud screech came from high up. Her eyes flicked open and she saw Ulrich pursued by three of the orbs, the four of them bursting out of the canopy and away into the sky. The white crow was nowhere to be seen.

She knew exactly what was going to happen next and despite her fear she didn't try to escape. The remaining orb rose up a little higher into the air. Then it dropped with great violence onto her chest. Her body jerked violently with the shock and then all was darkness.

16

AN UNLIKELY SOURCE

They were a motley crew, Hoagy thought, as he followed Esme and Jean at a discrete distance down the road to Moss Hill: the tall girl in purple beside the highly quaffed old lady. It had taken them a while to leave the flat because Esme had gone to quite bizarre amounts of trouble for the expedition.

The two-tone beehive was back in place, thanks to an inordinate quantity of hairspray (this architectural wonder had not been constructed for some time), liquid eyeliner had been applied with a precise little flick at the edge of each eye, and a dubious coral shade had been daubed upon the lips. Esme was nervous, too, and chain-smoked all the way.

'A filthy habit,' the cat grumbled to himself, which was his only option, as these two couldn't understand a word he said.

Finally, as they cut down a steep hill, Esme stubbed

out her half-smoked cigarette, placed it carefully in an old Altoids tin, and proceeded to pop two extra-strong mints into her mouth. The road had dipped right down and they were cutting up yet another steep hill when they turned into a secluded, gently sloping row of semi-detached houses with a view over far-away central London. Esme stopped in front of the neatest house on the street.

'We're here,' she whispered.

Jean was looking at the house. 'Le Crab really lives here? I sort of imagined she lived in a cave.'

'Sssh. And don't call her that. I'm sure she hates it. She is your headmistress, after all.' Esme smoothed her shirt and dabbed at the edges of her mouth in case any lipstick had smudged. It was like she was going in for detention herself, Hoagy thought a little contemptuously.

Jean still looked confused. 'I can't believe she actually exists outside of school. I'm just not sure it's possible.'

The old cat wound impatiently around Esme's legs and if she'd understood his mewlings, she would have heard him say, 'Could we please get on with it?' But despite the language barrier, she got the message.

'I know, dearie, I know.'

She took a deep breath and strode up the path that did not have a weed in sight, to the freshly painted dark-grey front door with its smart silver bell. Immaculate grey window boxes filled with geraniums stood attentively on guard and slatted wooden blinds were tightly shut at every window. Esme's index finger took ages to reach the bell, but finally it made contact and a shrill note rang out into the empty hall.

Eventually a dark figure, blurred by the frosted glass in the door, appeared and grew larger. Then a curt imperious voice asked, 'Who is there?'

Jean immediately tensed up and took a step back; Esme looked like she wanted to do the same, but held her ground.

'Muriel? I'm sorry to bother you. It's Esme. I wouldn't have come if it wasn't important.'

There was a long pause and then they heard a chain being removed, a couple of locks clicking, and finally the door opened to reveal Miss McCrab's stern white face. Wearing a floor-length black dress and a ruby red housecoat, she looked fairly terrifying. Though Hoagy could tell at once that she was no witch.

She took in the presence of Esme, one of her most frustrating and least obedient pupils, and a fat one-eyed old cat she didn't know standing on her doorstep, visiting her private abode deep into the summer holidays, with a frosty glance. 'What are you doing here?'

'Um, we, er, we need your help with something,' Esme spluttered.

Le Crab turned her attention to Jean. 'Jean Scott from Year Eight. I take it you haven't come by to discuss your end-of-term report? I thought we agreed to save that pleasure for September.'

Jean looked down but said, 'It's Maggie Blue. She's disappeared again.'

'Well call the police at once. What on earth are you thinking, Ms Durand?'

'Look, I don't think they can help. And it's Esme, as you know.'

'If the child is missing you must inform the authorities. I will do it for you if you don't act immediately . . .'

She broke off.

Esme was holding up the tiny bit of parchment they had found amongst Maggie's things. 'What is this? Do you know?'

Le Crab took it and her eyes flashed with strange energy. She glanced beyond them, as if worried what the neighbours would say.

'Come in, come in then, instead of causing all this fuss on the doorstep.'

They shuffled inside and the door was closed quickly behind them and locked once again, which Hoagy wasn't too happy about. He liked to have an escape route when he went into the houses of strange women, which frankly he'd done a lot of in his time, though normally in pursuit of fine cuts of meat. Esme and Jean took their shoes off without having to be asked, and even Hoagy wiped his paws carefully on the mat. He purred softly to himself as he looked around the hallway.

This headmistress was one tough old bird, but there

was something interesting behind the big disciplinarian act. Esme and Jean, too, were looking round with a certain wonderment.

The hall was painted midnight blue, tiny black and white tiles ran through it, and there were images on the walls of mountain ranges and deep dark forests. Le Crab ushered them into a front room that also seemed a million miles away from the faceless grey exterior.

In here the walls were covered in green velvet wallpaper and there were two enormous velvet couches in the same shade. There was no TV or radio, only a large desk covered in books and papers. The walls had hand-drawn maps in gilt frames and on various shelves there were curious shells, skulls, fossils and jagged clusters of quartz.

Le Crab offered no refreshments and though she sat at her own huge desk, she didn't offer anyone else a seat. She eyed Hoagy with deep irritation as he stretched out on her delightfully soft rug. He winked at her and purred deeply to try and annoy her further.

So she turned her attention away from him and drew her hands together on the desk. 'Where did you get this note?'

'It sounds odd, but the cat showed it to us.'

Hoagy found himself the recipient of another sharp look, during which he tried to eyeball her out again with his one eye. But surprisingly, the woman did not dismiss this suggestion out of hand.

'And you come to me, why?'

'Because . . . because you showed me something similar once, years ago, don't you remember? The language your father discovered. I think it's the same.'

Le Crab was staring at the note again and the atmosphere in the room felt very tense. Eventually she said, 'Yes, I recognise it. There was a time when I tried to learn the language myself, but I soon gave up.' She was no longer angry; the taut energy had drained out of her quite suddenly. The feeling that Hoagy sensed now was only sadness.

He could tell this change gave Esme a little hope and she pressed on.

'Last year Maggie Blue tried to tell me something about another world and I, well, I didn't really listen to her. Then when she came back the second time, she was too traumatised to speak about it. So I left it. I thought she would tell me when she was ready, except she never was.

'But she told Jean about this dark place she had to go to rescue the Beechwood girl. She said she gets there through a hole or something in Everfall Woods. We think she might have gone back.'

The woman's eyes were cold again. 'I have told my pupils over and over again not to go to Everfall Woods alone. Why won't they listen to me?' Le Crab put her head in her hands, as if exhausted by the subject. Then she looked up abruptly once more. 'So, what do you want from me?'

'I thought you might know something . . . anything. I'm desperate. What this note says, for instance.'

The woman got up abruptly and loomed over them all like a black column. 'You can leave now. I will let you know if I can help you, though I very much doubt it. Please do not come here again.'

They scrambled to get their shoes on in the hallway and then the door shut firmly behind them.

As they were all trudging back up the hill, Jean finally broke the silence. 'Is it just me, or has Le Crab got some major personal issues?'

She and Esme both burst out laughing. Hoagy didn't especially see what was so funny: the answer was clearly yes.

When Esme had stopped chuckling, she lit yet another cigarette and said, 'We shouldn't laugh, because really it's all to hide a lot of pain.'

'What pain?' Jean asked.

'Her father disappeared in the woods about thirty years ago. He was a scientist, a professor at King's, I believe. He used to disappear for days on end; it was quite normal apparently. But then he disappeared for good. She was a trainee teacher at the time.'

'You knew her then?'

'No, not then. But she told me about it.'

'So what happened?'

'Well, she was very close to her father. When he vanished

there were rumours that he'd gone off with another woman, but Muriel, I mean Ms McCrab, would never believe it. He disappeared totally and the last time he was seen he was going into Everfall Woods. She looked through his papers and found files of endless notes including a new language he was trying to decode.'

'How do you know all this then?' Jean asked.

'Well, we got rather close at one time.' Esme's voice wobbled a bit, but she quickly recovered. 'She's not all bad, you know. She was devastated at losing her father and she's never really got over it. She finds it hard to . . . to get close to people.'

Jean shrugged. 'She's got a cool collection of skulls.'

'True.'

'So, do you think she'll help us?'

Esme shook her head. 'I'm not sure. It was probably a mistake to take the note to her, but then she's the only one who could possibly help us. Well, as far as I know. I'm sure my friend Dot could have, but she's no longer with us.' She sighed then said quickly, 'Come on, let's go and have a cup of tea.'

Hours later, they were halfway through *City Slickers* on an especially grainy VCR tape, and Esme was snoring beside him, when the phone shattered the calm. Hoagy was up like a shot and Esme, too, was surprisingly rapid considering the amount of sherry she'd consumed during the film's first act. Jean, the purple-clad one, had left them some hours ago.

Esme staggered up and grabbed the phone. 'Yes?' she asked, a little breathlessly. There was a pause. 'You have? Hang on.' She scrabbled for the pen and paper by the phone. 'Hang on, OK.'

As she scribbled some notes down. Hoagy stood on the very tips of his hind legs to see what she was writing:

Greetings from . . . other world. [don't know] Something girl. [don't know] Help her.

'And then name?' Esme was saying. 'Oh, you think a symbol for a name. I see.'

Hoagy fell back onto the carpet in amazement. So perhaps the moon witch Dot had not been lying – she really had wanted the other witches to help Maggie.

Esme held the phone a little away from her face and gave him a thumbs up. As she did, the cat heard Miss McCrab's voice say, 'I always thought there was something special about Maggie Blue.'

And despite all her worries, the cat noted with satisfaction that Esme could not repress a smile.

17

THE STORM

The noise of the caged umons howling had woken him. Standing beside the maidservants, he'd watched as a guard carried the muddy and unconscious girl inside and up to the first floor. Then they'd all dispersed and Oz had returned to his tiny bedroom. Having finally fallen back to sleep, he'd dreamt of Maggie Blue all night.

He woke feeling confused and disorientated, and although he went to the forest, he had been drawn back to the house much earlier than usual. In the hallway he listened intently, but there was no sound and the place was deserted. He drifted down to the kitchen where he found several of the maids sitting huddled together. They stared at him when he came in, but did not move.

He drank some water, grabbed a piece of black wheat bread and walked back down to the main part of the house. Now, standing in the hall once again, he heard voices coming from upstairs. He crept up a few steps, but a guard immediately appeared and shooed him away. Oz scuttled back to his room, his heart pounding.

He sat on his bed wondering what to do. A series of images rolled mysteriously through his mind: his father sitting devotedly beside the sleeping woman; this same woman's calm and happy expression as she sat up and looked out over the iron-grey lake; the limp body of Maggie Blue being carried into the house; the orbs passing him without interest as they hovered along the corridors. These images did not seem connected but somehow he felt that they were. He stood up.

There was not a soul about as Oz crept stealthily round the outside of the house. Almarra's window was open. The sorcerer didn't feel the cold; in fact, she liked it. Oz assessed the building. It had been built for the heat in thick pale stone with large recessed windows and wide stone ledges. Warmth no longer existed here, but apparently it had done many moons ago. Using the thick ledge of the lowest window to push himself off, he shimmied up the stone pipe that allowed the water to flow from the gently sloping roof. He couldn't believe what he was doing, but his body obeyed him easily until he finally heaved himself right up onto the roof.

He tiptoed nimbly across it until Almarra's open window was directly below him. Voices reached him, but he couldn't hear what they were saying. He got down on his stomach and tentatively leant over the edge. At first he could only hear his own breath but gradually he tuned into the voices, though they were still faint.

Eldrow was speaking, 'How do we know you are telling us the truth?'

There was some giggling and whispering before one of the orbs spoke. 'We serve the Fathers, not you. It would be unwise to doubt us.'

'But they wanted her alive. What has changed their minds?'

There was more giggling and then another voice said, 'The girl has returned and so has the Great O, at the same moment.'

Almarra broke in, 'You know where the Great O is?'

'We can sense her – all shifters can.'

'If you had any real sorcerer power *you* would feel it too.' More giggling.

His father spoke again, 'So where is she?'

'We do not know exactly. But very close – we must act swiftly.'

Eldrow's voice was flat, 'What do you want from us?'

'Must we spell it out? It is likely the girl and the Great O are connected. If what the moon witches predict is true, then the girl will bring darkness, she is dangerous.'

'So you believe moon witches, do you?' Eldrow's voice was scornful. 'You must be desperate.'

'No, it is you who are desperate. Kill the girl before she reaches the Magic Mountains.'

'Why don't *you* kill her?'

'If you want to be welcomed into the City of Gold–.'

'Eldrow, what is wrong with you?' Almarra screeched. 'Of course we will end the girl.'

'If you fail, the Terrible Ones will deal with you.'

There was a polite meow and a smooth voice purred, 'Perhaps I could go to the Fathers and confirm their new orders? It would not take me long.' Oz recognised Cano's amber tones. He could picture the mountain cat's self-satisfied purple eyes turning to slits as he spoke.

'No!' cried Almarra. 'We have no time.'

More giggling, but Eldrow's voice was firm. 'We will wait until Cano returns.'

His father seemed to fear a trap, though Oz could not quite understand why. Still he was grateful . . . it gave him a chance. The orbs snickered and one said, 'As you wish. But it will only be the worse for you.'

Oz drew himself up, rolled onto his back and lay looking at the star-filled sky in disbelief. It was freezing but he stayed put, allowing himself to grow very cold – numbness was better than feeling. He wanted to disappear amidst the constellations, but after a long while, when it became clear that no such miraculous vanishing would take place, he sat up again and began to think.

So they were going to kill the girl without giving her a chance? Oz had not considered Maggie Blue as a real person until now, nor had he allowed himself to imagine what the Fathers might want with her. She had simply been their only way into the golden city – their only hope.

And he had no one in this world – not really. If he helped the girl to escape then everything would be lost, there would be no safety, nothing. But . . . he felt a connection to her. He had from the moment he'd caught a glimpse of her being carried into the house, small and limp, like a child, like him. Perhaps it was nothing more than that. Because he hated all the adults and he didn't see why they should be able to end her, just like that.

Besides, that golden palace, the hooded men and the dark pool all gave him the creeps. There was no real debate in his mind. For once, he was actually going to be brave, or try to be.

He sat up on his haunches and peered down to the ground below. There was still no one in sight, but he knew the creepy little boys might easily have shifted back into orbs and would find him out here. He needed to move fast.

He crawled over to the end of the house. Below him was a small round window like a porthole. Inside was where Maggie Blue had been locked in. He peered over the edge. The circular ledge might just be in reach, but there was really only one way to find out. It was the sort of thing that a moon ago he would never have dared try; but now he was sinewy and strong from all the climbing.

He took a deep breath then swung his body over the side, gripping fiercely onto the edge of the roof so that his knuckles turned white. He searched with his foot for the window. But he couldn't quite reach and for a few awful moments he just hung there, wildly wondering what to do.

But then his foot caught at a tiny ridge in the stonework, into which he just got a foothold. He pushed off it and flung his left foot at the round window ledge. He landed on it and managed to grip the top of the window with his hands. He stayed there, frozen like a statue, for several minutes before he dared to look down. It was a fair drop, but he thought he would survive, as long as he rolled away as soon as he hit the ground.

The thought soothed him slightly when suddenly a tiny white face appeared in the round porthole and tapped at the glass. Oz screamed and nearly lost his balance. The sound of his scream reverberated loudly into the still air and he expected to see the orbs or hear guards' footsteps. But nothing happened, nothing moved.

He started breathing again and found he was looking straight into the alert eyes of a small white bird. As he watched, the bird flew away from the window and hovered over the body of the girl, which it illuminated in a soft white light. He peered in through the glass. It was her: Maggie Blue was lying asleep or unconscious on a small couch. She looked very small and fragile, not like someone who could disrupt worlds. His dreams nagged at him in the back of his mind, but Oz couldn't remember them clearly. Only that she had been in them.

The bird returned to the window and the glow shone out onto Oz as he clung to every single particle of stone that he could. But the light was soothing. This shifter was unlike any he had encountered before: it was powerful, a little scary, and yet it calmed him. He found he could speak.

'They are planning to kill her. The Fathers have changed their minds.' The bird didn't react, so Oz carried on. 'Cano, the mountain cat, has gone to receive confirmation of their orders. When he returns, they will kill Maggie.'

The bird still did not react in any way and Oz worried it had not understood, or perhaps not heard him through the glass. Was it possible it wasn't a shifter after all? Had the girl brought it with her from another world? He tried again, louder this time: 'Can you hear me? They're going to kill Maggie Blue. You need to get her out.'

To his frustration, the bird flew away, but then it turned and flew back at full speed towards him. Oz slipped with the shock of it and just managed to grip onto the lower ledge as he fell back. The white bird clattered against the glass with its whole body. Surely it didn't think it was strong enough to break the glass? Oz manoeuvred his way down and, just as his foot made contact with the ground, there was a cracking sound and shards of glass shattered over him. He ran for cover, and when he looked up again, he saw the white bird screeching out of the jagged broken window and flying almost vertically up into the dull white sky.

The sound of the glass smashing was noticed and Oz heard shouts coming from within the house. But before anyone appeared, a deafening crack reverberated across the sky. The house, the lake, the trees – everything seemed to shake, as if reality itself was going to split apart. The umons howled, wild with fear. Dark grey clouds filled the sky and there were several thundering noises like the start of a great storm. Duly, rain began to fall, gently at first but then very heavily.

Oz sat and watched, stupefied, somehow unable to move a muscle. The sky closed in around him and the house and everything he could see. He was already soaked to the skin, but instead of finding shelter he felt the urge to lie back and close his eyes.

When he woke it was still raining and for several long moments he had no idea where he was or why. He could barely see a thing through the storm and his clothes were plastered to his body like a second skin. He was shivering uncontrollably. Then he remembered the white bird breaking through the glass and disappearing. Sure enough, there were shards of glass all over the ground and peering up he could just make out the smashed window.

He forced himself to get up and stagger round to the front of the house. There was a guard there, but he was lying on the ground and his axe had fallen uselessly beside him. Was he dead? Oz approached cautiously – but, to his astonishment, the huge man was only fast asleep. As if to confirm this, at that very moment he began to snore loudly. Was he drunk?

He went inside and stood dripping in the hallway. But apart from the steady drip-drip of water from his clothes on the stone, he couldn't hear anything else. Then he saw something, a dark heap at the top of the stairs. But it was only another guard, collapsed on the ground. He climbed up quietly, but it was the same thing – the man was fast asleep, sort of crumpled up as if he'd just fallen to the ground where he stood.

Taking courage, he stepped past him and opened the door into Almarra's room. The orbs had gone, but one maid and one guard were also on the ground. He moved into the sorcerer's chamber and, there on the bed, dribbling slightly, Almarra was splayed out, her magnificent red hair trailing around her. Edging towards her, still afraid she might wake up at any moment, Oz slipped the large set of keys from the chain she wore round her waist. He was so close to her that his hands trembled . . . but she didn't stir.

He rushed out and ran to the small locked door at the end of the passageway. It took a while but eventually he found the right key. When he opened the door, he found not one but two girls, both deeply asleep. He went up to the girl the white bird had illuminated, the one he knew was Maggie Blue without needing to be told. He shook her gently at first.

'Wake up! Wake up!'

Finally, after some more vigorous jostling, she came round. Her face was all squashed from sleeping too deeply and too long in the same place and an expression of profound confusion rippled over her features.

'Who are you?' she asked, yawning.

'Are you Maggie Blue?'

She looked at him with more focus. 'Yes. Who's asking?' But he didn't have time to answer because the girl suddenly let out a scream. 'Oh my God! *What* is Ida Beechwood doing here?'

18

RESCUE MISSION

After the chaotic battle at the portal, those that were still able flew to Sun City. Roda had not been seriously hurt, he only had a few scratches, but he was deeply humiliated . . . If anything, he seemed to be in a greater sort of pain than the injured shifters that were sprawled all around them in the great square.

They had lost Maggie Blue; that was the long and short of it. Shifters loyal to the Fathers had ambushed them, and they had lost the girl. Ulrich, once he'd recovered a little from the pain of the burns on his body from the orbs' attack, could only sit and wonder how they had been so naïve, so utterly stupid. But no answer readily presented itself. He even allowed himself to wonder at his master's mistake . . .

Much later, after the moon witches had attended to his wounds and dark-time had fallen, Ulrich was well enough to accompany Roda up to the top of one of the towers of the half-ruined fortress. It was a clear night and they could see across the dark velvety land by a waxing moon. All was still and quiet, and the desperate battle they had fought by the portal seemed like a bad dream. Neither of them spoke.

Zede appeared suddenly and without any sound: a tiny form in flowing black robes whose long white hair trailed far behind him on the ground. His purple eyes gleamed at them in the darkness. They were not allies exactly, but they had formed an uneasy truce in order to fight together against the Fathers, and to pass useful information to one another.

Without a glance at Ulrich, the ancient moon witch walked up to the great heron and faced him squarely. 'Why did you not tell us of the fortress being built in the Magic Mountains?' He spat greenish liquid onto the stones between them. 'Now we see why we are winning this war so easily. I thought we were united against the Fathers, at least.'

Roda bowed his long grey head respectfully. 'Because we still do not know if it really exists. We sent one of our best warriors to find out, but she never returned.'

Ulrich felt a pang of grief at the mention of the little wren. He had given up hope of ever seeing her again.

'And now I hear you have lost the girl? Of course, we want her dead. Perhaps someone else has taken care of it for us.'

Ulrich sensed the anger pulsing through his master,

but Roda showed no outward sign of it and responded in a calm flat voice. 'The Great O wants her alive. And we were ambushed, yes. The girl was taken.'

'And the Great O with her?'

'*She* was not taken,' Roda retorted. 'But she will not be parted from the girl.'

Zede nodded. 'Yes, so I understand. And you will still not tell us in what form the Great O has returned?'

Roda bowed his head. 'I am forbidden from doing so.'

'Hmmm. And what do you intend to do now?'

'We will stay here, if you allow, until Ulrich has fully recovered. Then, we will go in search of her.'

'We are already searching for her.' The ancient put his spindly translucent hands together and after a few moments of deep silence he said, 'Naturally you have heard of the previous ancient's vision? Of this girl bringing darkness?'

'Who doesn't know it?' Roda returned coldly.

'Indeed. I have seen something else this last moon. I was not sure whether to share it or not. I *think* it can't be true . . . but I *feel* that it is: the moon never lies to us.'

Beside him, Roda was very still and his face expressionless. But Ulrich noticed how Roda's long soft talons were gripping the stone beneath them as if he was fighting the urge to just take off and leave. The owl's own heart began to beat faster; why would this moon witch frighten him?

But all Roda said in the same flat voice was, 'What have you seen?'

'I still understand that the girl will bring darkness. She will be part of the destruction of the moon witches. We want her dead. In this we are against one another.'

'That's also no secret,' Roda said dryly.

'No. But now there is something new, and it is worse. I have . . . I don't know how to say it. I have seen that the girl is only a conduit; she is not the cause.' He paused. 'It is the Great O who wishes to destroy this world.'

For a moment no one moved or seemed to breathe. Then Roda unfolded his great wings and swung them threateningly at the witch, only a hair's breadth from his pale face. 'That is a vile untruth.'

Despite the fact that Roda could all too easily snap the witch's fragile body in half if he chose, Zede did not move a single muscle and said calmly, 'I only tell you what I have seen.'

Roda lowered his wings as Zede stepped back a little and bowed. But Ulrich caught the trace of a smile playing over the witch's repulsive white lips, and Roda noticed it too.

'Something amuses you?' the heron asked.

The sharp purple eyes fixed upon him once again. 'Not really. But if Mother Nature herself wants to destroy us then there is really nothing to be done except to laugh. We are all lost, even the Fathers in their golden tomb, if, as you say, it even exists. The war is pointless, everything is pointless and there is no victory for anyone.'

'If you have only just understood that you are winning an empty war then I pity you, but do not turn your self-hatred upon the Great O.' Roda's voice was steady again. He bowed then turned his back on the moon witch and took flight into the darkness. Ulrich followed him but he could feel those awful purple eyes boring a hole into his back.

They flew down from the fortress and landed in a corner of the great square. For a few moments Roda said nothing and the owl could still feel the horror and fear inside him. It disorientated him utterly. He was trying to form the words to ask what was wrong, when Roda turned to him and spoke low and urgently.

'We have to leave now. Have you the strength?'

The answer to this was clearly no, but he would never forsake his master. Ulrich did not mention the searing pain in his side. He only bowed his head and answered, 'I am with you.'

Not long afterwards he found himself flying over the vast waterways and forests of the Great Lakes where Roda believed Maggie could have been taken. Ulrich kept a little behind, pain shooting through his body at fairly regular intervals. But he was determined not to show weakness of any kind.

The white-time was bleeding into the darkness when he began to see a strange grey light looming on the horizon ahead. He called out to Roda, but the wind was just picking up and the heron didn't seem to hear. And then, quite suddenly, Ulrich found himself flying at speed towards a great grey vertical wall of cloud. He wheeled round before he collided with it. Roda too swerved and screeched out, and Ulrich followed him down to the forest floor where they both collapsed. Ulrich stayed on the ground, exhausted but alert: something unnatural was happening in this place. And he also sensed the Great O very strongly.

Down where they were amidst the trees, the dense grey air raged in front of them like a wall. Roda tried to pierce it with his beak, but he was thrown back. Ulrich tried to muscle his way in, but received the same treatment. The two birds got up and dusted themselves down.

'I've never seen anything like this,' Roda said.

'But what is it?' Ulrich asked.

'I don't know, but this is clearly the place we need to be.'

It was difficult to ask his next question. 'Do you believe what the moon witch told us? About the Great O?'

But Roda took off without answering. The faithful Ulrich followed him and they flew almost vertically up into the freezing air. Up and up, following the line of the storm that hid everything beyond it from view. Until finally they came to its peak and in the centre, to Ulrich's great amazement, was the white crow. It hung in the air, the storm emanating from its tiny white body, which was almost translucent.

Roda flew closer but the white crow seemed in a trance of some kind and he indicated that they should descend again. The owl nodded but his mind was scrambling to understand. What kind of emergency could have caused the Great O to take a risk like this? The strain of creating this storm must be weakening her severely; she looked about to break. It could only mean one thing: the girl was in extreme danger.

Ulrich was turning all this over in his mind when he heard Roda screeching harshly behind him once again. Ulrich followed the heron's stare: far below them, some distance away, two long dark snakes were moving swiftly over the land, black and awful as a nightmare: the Terrible Ones were coming.

19

ESCAPE

Maggie could not make sense of the information being flipped over onto the back of her eyeballs then turned the right way round again by her brain . . . it just couldn't be. For several long moments she stood motionless in the small room, her mouth wide open.

What her brain told her was that Ida Beechwood was curled up on a little bed, a fur blanket draped over her. Maggie's hand went to the small wound just behind her ear and touched the raised circle of damaged tissue there. Ida had one just the same: the scar they shared from their last time in the Dark World.

'What are you doing here?' she demanded, in a loud voice.

Her friend's eyes opened a little, but then just as quickly shut and she rolled over.

Maggie went up and shook her. 'What are you doing here?' she said again, louder this time. She was shocked by how angry she felt and she couldn't even explain it.

Ida sat up and rubbed her eyes. 'Hmmmn?'

Maggie could feel the little boy's powerful curiosity hovering just behind her, but she didn't care about him.

Ida looked around the room, reality dawning on her unpleasantly. Then she saw her. 'Oh my God, Maggie!' and she threw her arms around her and started to sob. 'I'm so relieved to see you.'

Maggie tried to bite back her irritation. She pushed Ida away but then she realised what must have happened. 'Did they force you to cross?'

Ida looked up. 'Who?'

Ida's curly hair was flat on one side of her head and her long eyelashes were thick from the tears. Despite everything, Maggie felt the usual lurch – she wished she could look beautiful like Ida, just once. But it was a truly dumb thought and she pushed it away again.

'The huge birds that cornered us in the street in West Minchen, remember? Did they make you cross over?'

Ida shook her head. 'No. I ran after you because I knew they'd take you to the same place in the woods, and I wanted to stop you going back. I thought they were going to kill you or something. So I tried to grab you, but you'd already gone through and I grabbed the owl instead and then I sort of fell through with it.'

'But where were you? I didn't see you.'

'I don't know, I passed out. When I woke up it was dark and these large ferrety things were lifting me out of the leaves and tying me up. They put me in a cart and dragged it along . . . And then I don't remember.'

'But why did you come?' Maggie asked, still incredulous.

She could tell this question annoyed Ida. Her friend sat up and pushed her hair out of her eyes. 'I didn't plan it. I thought you might actually need some help.'

Maggie said nothing, suddenly wanting to give her friend a big hug, but holding back.

'Who's he?' Ida was pointing to the small dark-haired boy who stood watching silently behind them. Maggie turned to look at him too and under their scrutiny he seemed to shrink back into himself. She realised she didn't know herself.

'I'm Oz.' He bowed slightly to them.

They couldn't help but giggle at his strange formal manner.

'Where are we?' Maggie asked.

'You are in a house in the Great Lakes.'

'Where's that?'

'We are close to the Magic Mountains and very close to the City of Flowers. But you are in danger and we have to leave at once.'

'And go where?' Maggie asked.

'The only place I know is Sun City.'

Ida frowned at him. 'Why should we do what you say?'

Maggie thought that was a good point. She looked back at the boy. He was agitated and despite herself she could feel his vulnerability. He was very scared and not doing a great job of hiding it. But what was he scared of? She vaguely remembered what had happened . . . the battle, the orbs . . .

'Are the orbs here?'

'Yes.'

'Who else?'

'There are guards, Almarra is here—'

'Almarra!'

'Yes, but I think she's asleep. At least she was a little while ago.'

'Asleep? What do you mean?'

'Um. There was this white crow with you.'

Of course! That's what was missing. 'Where is it now?' Maggie asked eagerly.

'I don't know exactly. I told it that they wanted to—' He stopped abruptly.

'Who wanted to do what?' Ida asked.

'Um, well, I mean I told it you were in danger. And it smashed the glass . . .'

Maggie turned and sure enough, the glass in a small round window had been shattered. 'Then what?'

'Then it flew off into the sky. And then this crazy storm started and since then everyone's been asleep.'

Maggie peered out at the dense grey air. It was true: rain was pelting down and she could see nothing out of the jagged broken window. The air was very cold. Why would the white crow want to make a storm like this? She closed her eyes, trying to feel a connection with it, but she couldn't feel anything. She suddenly felt afraid. She turned to the little boy and realised he could only be about nine or so.

'Do you live here?' she asked.

He seemed shocked by that. 'Oh no.'

'Then why are you here?'

'I was taken from Sun City.'

'Why?'

He looked uncomfortable. 'I don't know.'

Maggie exchanged a look with Ida. He was hiding something. She narrowed her eyes at him. 'Why should I trust you?'

He held up a set of large keys. 'If anyone else was awake, do you think they'd give me the keys?'

This was a fairly compelling argument; Maggie nodded. 'OK, so if Almarra is really fast asleep, you can show her to me. And you can go first.'

The boy nodded, trying to appear calm, but Maggie sensed his deep fear of the sorcerer. 'I'll take you to her.'

He led them out into the corridor. It was deserted save for a black figure slumped on the floor. Maggie stared at it . . . it seemed familiar somehow. She went up to it and realised it was one of the sorcerer's maidservants and, just as the little boy had said, she was deeply and unnaturally asleep. It was almost as if she had just slid down the wall.

Maggie bent down and touched the young woman's cheek: she was warm but the maidservant didn't flinch. 'One of these women saved my life,' she said softly.

They walked along past identical dark wooden doors until the boy stopped in front of larger double doors about halfway down the passage.

'Is this it?' Maggie whispered.

He nodded.

'You go in first,' Maggie said again under her breath and she shoved him forwards. The boy pushed the door open very slowly, then he stood back so she could see.

'Take a look,' he said.

Maggie edged cautiously past him.

The large room was empty save for a small stone pedestal, upon which various crystals and what looked like fern leaves had been placed like a shrine, and a large dark-wood bed covered in black drapes.

Collapsed in the centre of the bed, her red hair spooling unchecked around her, Almarra lay completely still, her eyes closed, her mouth slightly open . . .

Maggie turned back to the boy in astonishment. 'And she really can't wake up?' she whispered.

Oz shook his head. 'No, I don't think so.'

The girl broke into a smile. 'Good, I hate her.'

'Me too.'

Maggie looked at him in surprise and laughed. Then she went up to the woman on the bed.

'Hello? Almarra?' Maggie spoke very quietly. The woman did not move. 'Almarra?' she said again, louder. 'It's Maggie Blue here. Do you remember me? You told me how special I was.' Finally, she shouted right in her ear, 'ALMARRA! IT'S ME . . . MAGGIE BLUE!'

'Don't do that!' The boy stood a little way away looking scared again. But Maggie felt something dangerous rising in her.

'What are you doing?' Ida was watching her too, from the doorway.

But Maggie couldn't have very well answered her. She felt that crazy energy that she sometimes did, unstoppable; it was coursing through her at full speed. She jumped onto the bed beside the sorcerer and separated out two long ropes of Almarra's flame red hair. Then she tied them in a ridiculous knot on top of her head. She looked round for something else to do, but seeing as nothing obvious presented itself, she jumped down and kicked over the shrine so that all the crystals and greenery went flying across the floor.

'Don't!' cried the boy. 'It's bad luck.'

She looked at him more closely. 'You're still scared of her, aren't you? Even when she's unconscious.' Maggie leant suddenly against the wall; she felt dizzy. All her slightly mad energy drained away. 'Have you got anything to eat?'

*

164

The little boy fed and watered them as best he could. Then he found them two of the maidservants' black dresses. They were itchy and big, and when she and Ida looked at each other they burst out laughing and couldn't stop. And the boy looked so confused by their laughter that it made them laugh even more. When they'd finally calmed down, Oz, looking very relieved, led them down the stairs.

At the door, he disappeared for a few minutes, and when he returned, he handed Maggie a short, blunt-looking knife wrapped in a piece of thick leather.

He said, 'We might need to defend ourselves.'

Maggie didn't want to take it, but he was so serious that she thought it best not to argue and tucked it wordlessly into the pocket of her ridiculous dress before stepping out into the storm.

Now all Maggie could hear was the roar of the wind swirling around her. Visibility was almost nothing. She made it to the tree line and threw herself down, panting on the damp soil beside Oz.

'Did Ida make it?' she shouted into the wind.

'I'm here,' said an angry voice, as Ida collapsed onto the ground beside her.

Maggie looked back into the darkness and it was as if the house and the lake did not exist – the wind and the rain had swallowed everything up. Still, just to be safe, they crawled deeper into the forest before Oz dared to light his lantern.

Although it was more sheltered amidst the trees, the flame flickered erratically, and they all screamed as a round black shape loomed at them out of the darkness. In her fear, at first Maggie thought it was a wild animal, but then she saw it was a human leaning against a tree, slumped forwards, completely still, her face buried in the depths of her dress.

Oz approached tentatively, holding the flickering light up to her while keeping his distance. 'It's one of Almarra's maidservants,' he announced.

'How come she's awake?' Maggie asked, snatching the lantern from him and going right up to her.

'I'm not sure she is,' Oz replied.

'Do you think she was trying to escape?' Maggie bent down and shook her gently. After a while, the girl lifted up her face and blinked madly for a few seconds in the unexpected light.

She could only be a little older than Ida and Maggie. Perhaps she, too, was less affected by the storm than the adults. Her face was stained with tears, and her smooth black hair had fallen from its bun and half-hung around her face.

Maggie crouched down beside her. 'What happened?' she asked. 'Why are you here?'

The girl looked terrified and said nothing.

'The maids never speak,' Oz explained.

'Why not?' Maggie asked.

'I . . . I don't know,' Oz stammered.

On top of the boy's fragility, Maggie could now feel the girl's terror and her loneliness. And somewhere else, somewhere very high, she thought she could feel the fluttering presence of the white crow, but she might only be imagining it, wishing it. It was very faint. For a moment Maggie was overwhelmed. She didn't want to feel everyone else's feelings all the time: it was too much.

'Just SPEAK!' Maggie shouted.

The girl jumped and Maggie felt Ida's hand at her arm, drawing her back a little.

'Maybe she doesn't know how to talk,' Oz suggested in a whisper.

The girl looked resentfully at him with her large dark eyes. 'I know how to speak,' she said quietly. 'We're not allowed to.'

Her skin was sallow but shining, and she had a large mole that sat just above one corner of her lips. She was very beautiful, Maggie suddenly realised.

'How come you're out here?' Maggie asked her.

'I wanted to see if there was a way out.'

'Is anyone else awake?'

The girl shook her head. 'You can wake them up, but they are drowsy and useless, and then they go straight back to sleep.'

'And you're not affected?'

'I am. But not as much.'

Maggie noticed that she was shivering and she nodded at Oz who got out the fur blanket they'd taken from Ida's bed. 'You'll freeze out here. Why don't you go back?'

'I just can't seem to.' Then she stared at Maggie and suddenly grabbed her sleeve. 'You're the one they want, aren't you?'

Maggie moved away, trying to release her arm. 'Why do you say that?'

'Almarra said that if you got away, we'd all be punished, that the Terrible Ones would come and end us all. That we mustn't let you go.'

In the flickering lantern, Oz looked pale.

'Who are the Terrible Ones?' Maggie asked.

Oz said quietly, 'They are enormous black snakes or eels, or something. They serve the Fathers and it is said they can never die.'

'You've seen them?' The maid's voice was hushed with fear.

'Yes,' Oz replied. 'They didn't hurt me, but they terrified me all the same.'

'Where did you see them?' Maggie asked.

'In the Magic Mountains. The Fathers have built a palace . . .' He broke off.

He wasn't supposed to say that, Maggie thought. But why not? She knew there were things he was not telling her . . .

The maidservant's eyes had grown wide. 'The Terrible

Ones are most comfortable where there is the deepest sin – they bathe in it. If they find you, they will eat your soul.'

'And they are coming here? You're sure of it?' Maggie asked.

'I'm sure of nothing. It's only what I have heard, scraps. But if they come here they will kill every living creature they find,' she glanced resentfully at Maggie, 'even you.'

Maggie's heart lurched at this confident pronouncement of her death but she said defiantly, 'I won't be here.'

'You know a way out?' the girl asked hopefully.

'No, but I'll find one. I'm not planning to stick around and wait for a load of giant eels to get their teeth into me.'

Maggie felt a bubble of hysteria rising up in her at this ludicrous statement, but then she saw how afraid the girl looked and quelled it. She said with far more authority than she felt, 'Don't sit around here waiting. Take whatever you need and anyone else you can wake up and get to the edge of the storm. It has to stop at some point, and then at least you will have a head start. That's where we're going.'

The girl nodded, but Maggie felt sure she would not act. She was irritated by the maid's passivity and wanted to get away from the powerful waves of self-pity emanating from her.

When had she become so brutal? she wondered. She felt more, but she seemed to care less. Hadn't one of these maids saved her life, not so very long ago? Hiding Maggie in her huge skirts just before the awful Almarra pounced?

'You can come with us, if you come now,' she added, trying to be gentler.

But the girl shook her head. 'I may be able to wake some of my sisters,' she said.

Maggie nodded. 'Well, good luck.'

They all shook hands rather solemnly and then the three of them moved away into the deeper darkness of the trees.

'I hope she makes it,' Ida, who had been unusually quiet, suddenly whispered.

Maggie didn't even think the girl would manage to get up and walk back to the house; she would just sit there and wait for her fate to arrive. But she said nothing. It was not her problem.

Oz led them through the trees. As the wind picked up, his lantern wavered and finally blew out completely. But after a few moments they found they could just see enough to keep moving, the dense trunks of the trees somewhat darker than the rest. But it was slow progress.

The storm thundered and crackled around them, and the further they walked the more intense it seemed to get. It gave Maggie a headache. Every so often, small branches would crash down through the boughs onto the forest floor, and occasionally they passed a tree that had been entirely uprooted by the storm.

After a while Ida grabbed her arm and they walked along together, holding onto each other in their identical dresses, merging into the darkness as if they were one being, with little Oz leading the way. The trees were dense around them, moving together in the wind, swaying above them so violently it felt like they were looking up at a stormy sea, like they'd already drowned and were beneath the waves.

Maggie was starting to think that they would just keep walking along in this way for ever when Oz stopped and turned to them. It was so abrupt that they bundled into him.

'It's here,' he said.

Sure enough, Maggie began to see that there was a wall of dense grey-white air, lighter than the darkness, rising up in front of them. It formed a sheer wall that then arched back over the way they had come. Maggie let go of Ida's hand and moved closer. She could feel the wall of raging air almost pressing against her, powerful, desperate. It gave her the strangest sensation.

'There's no way through,' Oz shouted.

Ida stepped forwards, reached out impulsively and tried to thrust her arm through it, but she was thrown back and landed on the cold ground with a yelp. Maggie rushed over and helped her up.

It seemed foolish to follow in Ida's footsteps, but somehow Maggie couldn't help herself. She reached out her hand towards the billowing wall of air. But as the edge of her fingers touched it, she felt no especial resistance. Instead, it was like a thousand little pulses hammering at her skin, not painful exactly, but intense. She kept reaching her arm through, until suddenly she felt it come out the other side into clear air.

There was a violent jolt and then everything fell away with a huge hiss. The grey wall seemed to almost drop out of the sky, to dissolve, and the way was clear. The wind disappeared and at once everything was still. For a moment they all stood frozen in disbelief. Above the canopy, a nearly full moon, quivering and bright, was suddenly visible. And the deep silence rang in their ears.

'You did it!' Ida exclaimed behind her.

Oz stood beside her, a look of astonishment on his small worried face.

Maggie only shrugged, trying to hide the little curl of triumph she felt inside herself. But then something dropped onto her from the sky. She screamed and fell to the ground, half expecting to find a giant black eel writhing around trying to eat her soul. But instead, she saw the small white bird trembling in her arms.

'The white crow,' Ida said, wonder in her voice. 'It's still with you.'

Maggie felt overwhelmed by emotion; joy at seeing the bird once again. She could feel its warm delicate body in her arms, its tiny heart fluttering like crazy, pulsing with fear and exhaustion. Was it possible the bird had been protecting her all along? That it had created the storm?

She held it close for a moment. She felt tears coming – it

hadn't abandoned her; it would never leave her. But she pushed her tears back and recovered herself. She slipped the trembling bird into the pocket of the dress and shook her head at the curious glances of the other two. Then she turned and walked deeper into the forest.

20

THE WRONG PERSON

Ulrich had been on watch when it happened. The intensity of the storm had eased and he'd been able to see a little through the grey sheet of cloud and heavy rain. Then, quite suddenly, it had fallen away – vanished. The silence left behind seemed louder than the constant pounding of the wind and rain. For a few moments, the owl sat and stared, and his huge eyes opened a little wider.

Then he came to his senses and found Roda awake and alert beside him. They looked at each other and without a word took off into the dull white sky. Almost at once, Ulrich saw beneath them a huge placid lake and beside it a two-storey stone house. To the west, the awful black slithering bodies were closer, though they still had to make it through the western forests; and with a screech, Ulrich brought his master's attention to the east where a rippling dark phalanx moved through the trees: the moon witches were also coming this way. They needed to move fast.

Below them, the previously deserted scene had become a hive of frenzied activity. Guards ran in and out, umons, apparently trapped somewhere behind the house, were howling, and just emerging by the lake, unshaven and dishevelled, they saw Eldrow. Roda screeched beside him and when Ulrich glanced over, his master's eyes were quite wild.

'Do you think Maggie's inside?' he called out.

But Roda did not answer. He wheeled round and up, and went into a dive. The owl watched as the great heron slammed at speed into the unsuspecting human below. Eldrow screamed in shock and fell to the ground.

Roda was on top of him. 'Where is Maggie Blue?'

Cowering, Eldrow held his hands to his face to try and protect himself. 'She's gone. She was here before the storm . . . now she's gone.'

'You're lying! Where is she?'

'I swear to you, it's the truth. She must have gone when we were all asleep.'

Roda did not wait for further denials. He raised one huge wing in the air and whacked the man on the side of his head. Eldrow fell back and as Ulrich landed beside the body, he saw a slow trickle of blood seeping out of the man's ear.

He looked uncomprehendingly at his master. It was not like him to be so violent without cause. But this was not the time to ask questions. They went down a small path that led to an underground level of the house and found themselves in a narrow windowless corridor lit by lanterns. Roda moved purposefully ahead and he followed him into a small cell. Here, the woman he had seen taken from Milton Lodge, Maggie Blue's mother, was lying motionless under a white cover. She was unconscious and her breath was slow and shallow.

Ulrich expected to immediately move on and keep searching, but to his confusion his master remained still, his eyes fixed upon the woman. Then he swept the blanket off and swooped up the limp human body.

Ulrich stared, aghast. 'What are you doing?'

'What does it look like?' Roda replied angrily. 'I'm getting her out of here. She will be annihilated.'

'But why would . . . ?' Ulrich began, but Roda shoved past him. Ulrich followed him back up to the lake and was immediately aware of a strange humming. It was faint but it filled the air and reverberated in his ears.

Roda's face was set and grim. 'The Terrible Ones,' he said.

There was a patch of blood on the ground where the heron had attacked Eldrow, but the man's body had gone. Had someone come to help? Had he died and the body had been taken already? But Ulrich soon forgot about it, because across the eerily still water of the lake, three balls of light were moving towards them at speed.

Roda laid the unconscious woman down on the ground behind them with infinite care and then nodded at Ulrich who nodded back – he knew the drill. He just didn't understand why they were bothering to protect this useless human being.

The thick feathers on the owl's wings tingled unpleasantly – he had a sense of foreboding. Something was wrong, but he could not quite grasp what it was. What he did know, without doubt, was that they should be searching for Maggie Blue in every corner of this place; that they should be saving her at all costs. But his warrior brain pushed these concerns aside. In the face of violent conflict, he had been trained these many moons to focus on nothing but the present; never to let emotion dictate or get in the way of action. And action was close at hand.

Sometimes the worst part of a battle was the dead moments just before the explosion of violence, and Ulrich felt that quiver of fear now. But then the heron pushed himself up into the churning sky and Ulrich followed. His wings felt unbearably heavy, all the fatigue and his injuries were starting to tell, but he forced his way up by sheer determination. The two birds hovered there in the sky for a moment until Roda uttered the words that Ulrich had been dreaming of for so many moons, 'Attack!'

He pushed his wings hard into his body and dived, Roda at his side, and for a moment all he felt was happiness and exhilaration. The orbs scattered, howling and shrieking wildly. Ulrich pulled up just above the water, but now the orbs were attacking from above, dropping at speed. Ulrich brushed them aside with his great wings, though the pain of the electrical shocks was excruciating; they burned and singed his flesh where he had already been burned.

This was how the orbs fought, he knew: by ducking and diving, by exhausting their enemies. They must try and keep the fight over the water: it would not end them, but falling in the lake would force the orbs out of the fight for some time.

Ulrich dragged himself up again to prepare for another assault, and watched as Roda's powerful wings dashed two of the orbs into the water where they instantly shifted into the yellow-eyed boys, spitting and yelping as they swam for shore. The remaining opponent hovered over the water for a moment, taking stock of the situation, then fled.

Ulrich flew back to the ground to catch his breath. But the humming was growing louder and louder, and from the other side of the forest they heard the wails and whoops of the moon witches.

Roda's face was grim. 'Go and release the umons,' he commanded.

'But . . .' Ulrich forced it out this time. 'But what about the girl? We have to find her.'

'She's long gone. And the white crow too. Can't you feel that? They're no longer here.'

'Then what are we doing here?'

Rage flickered in the heron's yellow eyes. 'Do you dare to disobey me?'

Ulrich bowed his head deferentially.

'Release the umons at once.'

Following the sounds of their howls, Ulrich flew round to the back of the house and found two low buildings where the creatures were imprisoned. At the same moment, guards were running for one of the buildings, evidently intending to harness the umons to a large cart that other guards and maidservants were hastily filling with supplies. Ulrich shook his great head – if they knew the Terrible Ones were coming, they wouldn't be worrying about possessions. Then again, maybe they would – you could never predict how stupid humans could be.

As he landed, he shifted into human form, and brushed the guards aside with one sweep of his great arms. The door was locked and though he was tempted to engage in a bit of door battering – one of his hobbies – for once he took the less dramatic method and simply unhooked the key from one of the guard's belts.

The umons came streaming out, howling and wailing. They knew, Ulrich thought, they understood. He moved over to the other low building and released the remaining captives. The creatures streamed into the woods, running for their lives.

He turned to retrace his steps back to Roda when he saw Almarra. She was standing beside the house; her hands were over her ears and she was screaming. She noticed him and turned her terrified eyes towards him. She stretched out her spindly arms.

'Please!' she cried. 'Please, help me! Don't leave me here.'

But Ulrich turned away. He could still hear her pleading voice behind him as he started running and shifted just as he left the ground. He flew back to Roda, who heaved the unconscious woman onto his back and joined him in the sky. The humming noise was almost unbearable now, hammering in their inner ears so that it was hard to keep flying straight.

They'd just reached the forest when they heard the most unearthly scream. He knew it was Almarra and it shook the very leaves on the trees. But he didn't look back. Below them they began to see the first moon witches breaking through the trees.

'Go back!' Roda screeched imperiously down to them. 'The Terrible Ones are here! Go back! Get back!'

Some of the witches stopped and stared up at them. There seemed to be confusion about what to do. Roda kept screaming down at them. But the two birds did not stop. Nothing in this world could have made Ulrich stop. The terror he felt was worse than anything he'd experienced before. All that mattered was that they got away from this evil, this darkness that would crush the life out of everything.

21

THE FIGHT

The owl didn't know how long they'd been flying. He only knew that he was devastated by exhaustion. Ahead of him, Roda was still doggedly fighting through the air. The woman had woken up and was desperately clinging to his back. And now they were finally dropping down through a heavy mist into a valley he had never seen before.

Roda collapsed beside another vast lake, and the woman tumbled off him. Ulrich landed a little way from them and pressed his face into the cool mossy grass.

He must have passed out because when he woke the dark-time had fallen and he was frozen to the core. He managed to get up, ruffled his feathers violently and inspected his new wounds. Then he looked around him and gradually his huge eyes began to see . . . A large beautiful lake flanked by cliffs of pink stone, and beyond and above them, land that rose up into a looming darkness that he could not permeate.

Almost at the top of the cliff face, a small fire was burning insistently, its blue-orange flames licking up into the night. He flew up, his wings horribly stiff from the cold, until he was close to the fire. It was in the mouth of a small cave that had been bored out of the rock face, by nature or otherwise he could not tell. He hovered closer.

To his horror he saw two human bodies intertwined – a man and a woman. The man had blue-grey hair and slender wrists; the woman was also very thin, very pale and she was wrapped in a thick white robe. The firelight flickered over their sleeping faces. Ulrich felt bile coming up his gullet and flooding into his bill. It was disgusting; it was wrong. There must be some logical explanation, some reason why Roda was doing this. Perhaps he was tricking the woman, getting information out of her? He prayed to the moons that it was so.

Like every shifter, Ulrich knew that relations between humans and shifters were strictly forbidden. Too much contact with the endlessly manipulative and emotionally fallible human beings fatally weakened warrior shifters. No weakness could be allowed; no feelings could be allowed. So it had always been. Those who disobeyed were treated to the harshest penalties . . . on both sides. Those who disobeyed were outcasts . . . lepers. He turned and flew at speed into the forest to take refuge, hoping that somehow it was all a bad dream.

*

When the white-time broke through, Ulrich roused himself from the shelter of the ancient oak tree and flew up into the air, purposefully not turning his eyes to the scene of the night before. He needed to clear his mind.

The mist had lifted and when he flew up beyond the cliffs and over the fertile uneven ground, he saw the Magic Mountains in the distance. His heart swelled to see his old home, looking from here as if nothing at all was wrong. He flew over the mountainside, rising towards the caldera. The air was pure here and as he wheeled over the verdant moss and boiling pools of water, he almost forgot his fears.

At the top he saw below him the electric blue of the acid pool that had formed in the heart of the imploded volcano. It was a beautiful sight and for a moment it stilled some of the violent anguish in his heart. But when he turned back to survey the huge lake far below, he saw a figure at its edge and all the dread and anger returned.

He tracked back down the mountain until he found a small stream of pure water trickling past the edge of the forest. He drank his fill then flew round to the lake. His master had returned to the narrow plateau in front of the small cave. Roda was still in his unfamiliar human form: it was not a good sign. He did not look up or speak as Ulrich landed beside him.

Eventually Ulrich broke the silence. 'What is happening?'

Roda finally looked at him and smiled. 'Nothing at all.'

Rage began boiling in Ulrich's veins, but he managed

to control himself enough to say, 'We have to find the girl. I don't understand what we are doing here,' he looked at the woman still asleep in the purplish innards of the cave, 'with *that*.'

Finally something flared in the eyes of the passive young man, but he still said nothing.

The lack of action, of activity or orders made Ulrich feel as if he was going mad. 'We have to do something!' he burst out.

'What do you suggest?'

Ulrich's glaring eyes flickered manically between Roda and the woman. 'Why are you protecting her?'

Roda ignored the question. 'What Zede told us . . . about the Great O wanting to destroy the world, not save it.'

'That's a lie.'

'I don't think it is. I believe him.'

Ulrich sat open-beaked. For a moment the world reeled and he felt himself losing his grip, felt he might topple off the edge of the cliff and crash down into the water below. But he gathered himself and looked with disgust at the sleeping human. 'What is wrong with you?'

To his great horror, his master smiled again. 'I have committed my first act of rebellion – I recommend it to you, my faithful acolyte. And it is true that many moons ago I fell in love with this human . . . And I see it disgusts you.'

Ulrich could hardly deny it. He wretched up a small bitter pellet that he spat over the edge of the cliff.

'I was told, and gladly believed, that she was dead. And when I saw her again, I wished that she were dead. I dreamt of killing her myself. But now, when I realise we are all going to die anyway, things have changed.'

He laughed and in a way Ulrich did not recognise. The thought flickered through his mind that his master really had gone mad.

'I rescued her from the Terrible Ones. She did not deserve that. As to our daughter Maggie Blue, her fate is no longer in my hands.'

Ulrich gasped for air. His talons gripped the pink rock so hard that they made an impression. There was only one thing he knew in the face of chaos and as he thought of it, his breathing returned to normal and his vision steadied.

After a moment or two, his cold hunter's eyes drifted over Roda's body from head to toe. 'But perhaps I can still be of assistance to you, my master,' he said in a steady voice.

From nothing he turned on the speed, tore past Roda into the cave, talons raised. He flew straight at the sleeping woman curled up on the ground, going for her neck. But, as always, Roda had read him and before he could make contact with that pathetic limp flesh he was slammed against the back wall of the cave. He screeched in pain and lay winded for a moment. The heron, because it was the heron now, stayed very still, silhouetted against the mouth of the cave.

The owl took it all in then rolled his eyes back into his head, pretending to have fallen unconscious with the impact. He took a few deep breaths and then flew as fast as he could out into the clear air. The heron screamed with rage and chased after him.

As Roda climbed higher above him, Ulrich zigzagged in the air to put him off. But the heron turned downwards, his body shaped like an arrow, and with deadly speed descended. He anticipated Ulrich's next move and struck him brutally on the back so that the great owl tumbled out of the sky. As he lay on the ground whimpering, Roda went into a full dive, but the owl swerved at the last moment so that Roda hit the ground hard and cried out.

Ulrich scrambled his body round to make sure he got back up into the air and at once he understood what was unthinkable – this was a fight to the death. He may have struck the last blow, but both shifters knew that it was Ulrich who was the most afraid, who most wanted to fly away. The knowledge fizzled between them.

He darted to his left and flew as hard as he could across the expanse of water. But he soon realised he had gambled wrong. The distance was greater than he had calculated in his panic, and he could feel the blue shadow closing in on him.

He was only about halfway across the lake when one of the heron's powerful wings struck him. The blow knocked him off his flight path and he span away, but it did not completely derail him. He managed to keep flying, and

Roda had to recover from the effort of the attack. But then he was upon him again.

This time, trying to take the heron by surprise, Ulrich flipped his body over whilst flying at speed and tried to rip a piece out of Roda's belly as he attacked. But his talons missed and instead he felt the heron's huge wings wrap about him, suffocate him. He was falling, wrapped in the huge wings that held him tight, strangling his ability to fly.

Ulrich fought with all his might, scratching and pecking, trying to tear at the flesh beneath the layers of feathers with his beak and escape, but Roda held him tight. Ulrich heard him scream, a wild screech of triumph, but the sound was lost as he smashed into the freezing water. He plunged in deep with the impact.

As the momentum began to slow, he thought to open his wings and try at least to push himself back up to the top. But then another more extreme idea entered his freezing mind. Instead of opening up, he tried to keep his speed of descent going. He blew any remaining air out of his lungs, tucked his great head into his chest, and pressed his wings tightly round his body.

To his relief, he kept going down, he kept drowning. Eventually, eventually he must come to the bottom. For a moment he stopped believing, but then his talons hit a layer of soil. He dug them in as fast as he could and with a Herculean effort, he shifted, though it felt like he did it with heavy stones pressing down against him.

Freed from his waterlogged and utterly useless feathers, he pushed himself off and swam powerfully back to the surface then burst out, gasping and gulping the air. He knew Roda would be watching him; that he would never leave the scene until a kill had been fully administered.

Strangely the heron did not attack immediately so he was able to make it back to shore, every limb impossibly heavy, every breath rasping in his lungs. Perhaps Roda was struggling to find the energy too. The great owl-man dragged himself up onto the muddy banks and lay there for a moment half-dead.

But no, Roda had only been waiting for a clean shot at him, because the heron was upon him again. Ulrich tried to roll out of the way, but he wasn't fast enough. The grey bird drew the dagger of its beak and thrust it into his stomach. Ulrich cried out in such agony that he sensed Roda hesitate.

Or was it because his scream merged with another? And the woman's continued long after his?

'Stoooooppppppp!' she screamed.

With blurry vision he turned and saw her standing outside the cave.

The heron looked over at her, blood dripping from his beak.

'Stoooppppp!' came her wild scream again.

Ulrich had seen Roda deliver the final blow often enough to know there would be no second chances. Blood seeping from his wrecked body, he somehow managed to get up and run for the trees.

He flung himself amidst the dead leaves, into the relieving darkness and dampness. For several moments he lay on the ground, panting. His heart was beating in a way that terrified him. But what did not terrify him now? Everything was over. Meaning disintegrated before him; there was not a single thing that made sense. He felt separate from his body, away from the searing pain that he observed as if from somewhere in the sky above him.

He considered Roda's strange words about rebellion. He could feel his blood still seeping into the ground, the earth of his homeland. At that moment he resolved that, if he survived, he would cross through the portal near Sun City and return to the other world. He would make for that peaceful garden in which he had longed for the battle, but which now seemed a paradise, a sanctuary, where the sunlight beat down and nothing at all happened. From that curious bucolic spot he would decide what to do, or if, in fact, there was anything he could do at all.

22

UNEXPECTED GUEST

Esme was stretched out across two chairs in full sun. Hoagy, after mewling pathetically for half an hour or so, had gone to sleep in the shade of her reclining body.

It was about eleven o'clock in the morning, and she wasn't exactly proud that this glorious summer day found her still in her dressing gown, her huge sunglasses glued to her face, a glass of brandy in one hand. Nor did it please her that her hair was a mess, that she could smell burnt toast, and that the phone had rung three times and she hadn't bothered to answer it.

It was a few days since Miss McCrab had half-translated the curious note. It had seemed exciting at the time, but Esme had realised they were just as stuck as before. She didn't have any more ideas.

Ever since Dot's body had been discovered, she had been struggling; and now Maggie had disappeared again, and Cynthia too. She didn't have the strength to even think about these things any more. She just wanted to lie here and forget about everything, to drift away in the haze of the sun.

'Um, excuse me? Aunt Esme?'

The voice was right beside her ear and she jumped a mile. The brandy flew from her hand and the glass shattered on the weed-infested path.

'Drinking spirits in the morning?' the voice continued. 'Not a good move.'

Esme pushed up her sunglasses to see who on this earth was bothering her. She saw Jean standing there: tall, gangly and horribly eager.

'I tried calling,' the girl explained. She looked down at the shattered glass. 'I'll clear that up.'

She disappeared and a few minutes later returned with some old newspaper and began carefully gathering up the broken glass. Esme lay back and watched the girl pick up every sliver and fragment of glass. It was calming to see someone doing something properly round here. By the time Jean had gone round to deposit it in the recycling bin, Esme felt somewhat soothed. Secretly she was glad the glass had dropped on the ground – its contents were not destined to make her feel better.

But when Jean returned and stood staring at her, all energy and youth, she once again felt like slumping back and conking out. Hoagy began to mewl plaintively beneath her and she suddenly realised what was wrong.

'You wouldn't feed the cat, would you? He'll eat anything.'

The girl shrugged and was gone again, Hoagy trailing in her wake.

Esme sighed with satisfaction. This master plan had killed two birds with one stone, for a minute or two at least. In fact, it seemed quite a while and she had just about dozed off when something blocked out the sun.

'Why are you being like this?' Jean sounded angry.

Esme propped herself up on her elbows. 'Like what?' she asked, genuinely confused.

'So . . . so lazy. Shouldn't we be trying to find Maggie? Shouldn't we be springing into action?'

'Springing into action?'

'Maggie has gone to this other world. Or I mean, she probably has.'

'So?'

'So shouldn't we be doing something?'

'What do you suggest, dearie?'

'Well, I mean, we need to find where this other place is.'

'I tell you what, when you've found where this other world is, you come and wake me up, all right?'

'Um . . . I . . .' The girl moved away.

Esme pushed up her sunglasses and rubbed her eyes. 'I'm sorry, dearie. Forgive me. Muriel, I mean Miss McCrab always makes me feel low.' She'd barely realised that this was affecting her too, and she certainly didn't know why she was telling Jean.

'Why?'

'We . . . well, we used to be close.'

'You were in love with Le Crab!?' The girl was openly laughing at the very idea.

'Ssshhh, no nothing like that. Well, something like that.'

'So what happened?'

'Oh, not much. She doesn't like letting her guard down. Not since her father disappeared in the woods. And now, if I see her at all, which is rare, I can assure you, she treats me like some unwelcome admin assistant.'

'Oh.'

'But, dearie, really, forget all that. What can we do about Maggie? I have no idea. I've lived here for years; I've walked every inch of Everfall Woods and I have never found another world. She has gone somewhere and we can't help her. That's why I'm drinking brandy at eleven in the morning, if you must know. Because there is nothing we can do.

'I should have listened to her when she tried to tell me what was happening – months ago. But I didn't, you see, and now there's nothing to be done. It's my fault.'

She stopped talking, exhausted. She hadn't felt this low for a long time, for years. She didn't want to sink into the depths again – the idea of it was always lingering in the back of her mind and it scared her.

She wished her friend Dot was here to help. But she had been brutally murdered for no reason; senseless wrecking violence that Esme could not begin to make sense of. Everything was falling apart. She felt ashamed, but she couldn't help it – she began to sob.

When Esme looked up again, she saw that Jean's face had frozen in horror, which cheered her up a bit. It always fascinated her when people were frightened of crying . . . it was the sign of an emotionally repressed upbringing. She looked at the girl with a little more interest.

But her amateur psychoanalysis was brought to a halt by Hoagy, who had returned from his feed and swiftly began a new mewling performance. He was standing at the side of the house, his tail flicking from side to side, and he was making the most appalling racket.

'What on earth is it now?' Esme said irritably

She hauled herself up. But there was nothing to be seen down the narrow side passage that led back to the road. As she peered down, the cat began to rush towards the road, his tail held high.

'He wants us to follow, don't you think?' Jean suggested, just behind her.

'Really?' Esme said, feeling all heavy again. 'Can I at least get out of my dressing gown first?'

Hoagy sat for at least fifteen minutes, his most sardonic expression set on his round face, as Esme dressed and got her hair into some kind of order. Jean sat in the sunshine, biting her nails and bouncing her leg up and down in a way that drove the cat close to the brink, until finally Esme emerged.

Hoagy immediately disappeared and the humans followed him down the cool passage. He trotted to the end of the driveway and disappeared to the right. Esme and Jean hurried to the pavement and saw him already halfway down the road.

The cat always kept about ten feet in front of them, jumping onto walls, spraying wee at unsuspecting shrubs, and rubbing himself violently against lampposts – old habits died hard, after all. He turned down Church Vale and Esme realised that, of course, he was taking them to Everfall Woods.

After the heat and glare of the streets, the woods in West Minchen were amazingly cool and very empty. They only saw one old man clutching a bottle in a paper bag, a doleful Alsatian sitting beside him.

'He's harmless,' the man called out drunkenly. 'He won't hurt you.'

Esme looked at the trees more closely than she ever had, and for the first time their beauty amazed her – the beech, ash and hazel, and the ancient oaks all in full leaf. High above them, the leaves mixed and dappled so that the canopy looked like a network of fine lace. Off the main paths, in the heart of the trees you could almost imagine you were in another world. But imagining was no longer enough, Esme thought. It seemed strange that Dot had died here . . . or at least her body had been abandoned here. To have been left so near the enormous Victorian grave-yard, but not buried, was not right. She shuddered.

And this was all a bit crazy, even by her standards. When she'd been very down, she'd tried everything: goat yoga, organic hormones, chakra meditation, crystal cleansing . . . but following an old one-eyed cat into the woods in search of a doorway into another world – this really was the pinnacle of her 'hippy tendencies', as Muriel had always referred to them. But she felt a little better for getting up and doing something – the gangly energetic girl had been right about that at least.

The cat stopped in the middle of a copse, beside a particularly gnarled old tree that had somehow survived the general cull to make way for new growth. It was bent over and had formed a sort of archway. Hoagy sat beside it and fixed them with a particularly intense stare. Esme and Jean climbed over the low fence made of old sticks and branches and joined him.

'Is this the place?' Esme asked.

The cat responded by purring very loudly.

'This is the place where Maggie's gone?'

Again the cat purred like a motorbike. It was surprisingly easy to communicate with him, Esme mused.

'Ida Beechwood disappeared round here,' Jean whispered, right beside her. 'Some people said it was Satan worshippers and stuff.'

Esme looked round. It was just a cleared area in the middle of the woods where new saplings were pushing through. Ground elder, thorns and nettles were rampant, some ferns grew, and little birds hopped in and out of sight. Above them, a lone squirrel chittered manically, its tail twitching. But there were no other-worldly signs, no wardrobes, secret doors or mysterious symbols – things you tended to look out for when crossing to parallel universes.

After a while, Esme said, 'So, what do we do?'

In answer to this question, Jean spent several minutes rustling around in the undergrowth, inspecting holes and hollows in nearby trees and, Esme supposed, generally looking for handy doorways into other realities.

But now her long dark fingers twined themselves together. 'Um . . .' Then the fingers flew apart and began snapping twigs of saplings and ripping leaves off nearby branches. Her leg was jiggling again. 'Um, I don't really know.'

Esme sighed and sat down on a fallen log. Jean kept bouncing around: the girl was simply incapable of keeping still for ten seconds. The cat, meanwhile, had settled in a small patch of dappled shade and had his one eye half-closed.

Maybe this was the place Ida had disappeared, and Maggie too. But how did it help? Esme began to feel the wearying depression that had plagued her for the last few days sink over her once more. And then she thought about the glass of brandy she'd been holding – perhaps it would have been best to drink it after all, and then another one straight afterwards, too. Abruptly, that was all she cared about.

She stood up – she must get home as quickly as possible and get some drink down her. Why had she ever been talked into this? She was just forming the words to tell Jean that she was leaving when something enormous shot past her and landed with an almighty bump a few feet away on the floor of the copse.

Esme screamed and was vaguely aware of Jean's cries mingling with her own. But Hoagy, the old streetfighter, was unfazed, and immediately pounced. That was what she saw when her fear passed a little and she could focus again: the old cat sitting territorially on top of an enormous grey bird.

'It came out of nowhere!' Jean shrieked, leaping around beside her,

Esme gasped – its feathers were all glutinous with dark blood, and the bird was moaning or crying, the noise issuing from the side of its sharp curved beak.

Esme and Jean edged towards it. It was a grey owl, and a magnificent one, or had been. There was a deep slash in its belly and its breath was coming in sharp shallow puffs. It was clearly dying.

'Is it dead?' Jean asked.

'Not quite,' Esme whispered. She felt unnerved by the

bird's presence; it did not look normal. Something strange had entered the atmosphere and the air itself seemed colder. She shivered.

Hoagy hadn't moved, as if terrified the bird would try and fly off. But Esme didn't think there was too much chance of that . . . Then something very odd happened . . . or seemed to happen.

The cat strained his neck forwards and began to make a serious of low purrs and mewling noises right in the owl's face. And even weirder, the owl's beak seemed to be moving very slightly in response.

Jean finished her thought. 'Are they *talking*?'

Esme shook her head. 'I've absolutely no idea, dearie.'

But Jean was already hopping from foot to foot in excitement. 'No, I really think they are. They're communicating somehow.'

Could the wretched girl just stop dancing about for a moment?

The two humans waited dumbly until whatever it was, was over. Then Hoagy's head shot up and, glaring at them with a strange intensity, he beckoned them with one paw. As they came closer, the owl managed to jerk its head round and Esme saw two fearsome eyes glaring out of the huge feathered grey head.

The cat now wrapped its forepaws around the bird's body and made as if to carry it.

'You want us to take him?' Esme intuited.

The cat purred vigorously.

'Where? The vets?'

A sharp hiss.

'To Milton Lodge?'

Again the cat purred enthusiastically. And Esme felt like she was in a dream, a surreal and very long dream, probably brought on by excess alcohol consumption and too much sun. But as she couldn't get out of it for now, she'd just have to carry on until she woke up.

'Can it help us find Maggie?' Jean asked, and this got the cat really excited – he nodded and purred this time, and his tail managed to flicker about all at the same time. She seemed to have hit the jackpot there.

Esme and Jean looked at each other, and disbelief was in both their eyes.

'How will we carry it?' Jean asked.

'If I'd known I'd be lifting gigantic bleeding owls about, I would have brought my shopping trolley,' Esme remarked grimly.

'I could run back and get it,' Jean suggested.

But the cat was having none of this. He started hissing and his tail flickered angrily from side to side now.

Esme rolled her eyes. 'Fine, fine. It seems we don't have time for that. Here,' she slipped off her navy blazer, 'maybe we could sort of roll it up in this?'

They managed to get the coat round half of it. They rolled it onto its side and the two odd grey furry feet lolled.

Its eyes had closed. Perhaps it was already dead, Esme thought dully, watching its thick blood soak into her blazer lining.

The two humans tried to lift it, but it was not possible. This was larger and heavier than any normal bird, even a large bird of prey. Again Esme felt a sliver of cold enter her, a fear – the bird was unnatural, other.

This time, however, they could put Jean's endless energy to use. 'There's an old rusty wheelbarrow in the back garden at Milton,' Esme told her. 'I think it'll just about hold this thing. Grab some coats and blankets,' she added, handing the girl the key.

Once Jean had dashed off, Esme and Hoagy sat there in a silence only punctuated by the shallow ragged breath of the dying bird. Around them she could hear a few screams from kids and occasionally a dog sauntered past, its owner a little further away, keeping to the paths. If anyone asked, Esme didn't have the strength to think up a reason for what was going on. But luckily the dog walkers didn't come close and were looking at their phones anyway.

Finally, they saw Jean running back through the trees, the decrepit wheelbarrow bumping violently over the roots and dips in the forest floor. She barely seemed to be out of breath and she had also brought two cushions from the garden. They would have to do.

It took all their strength to get the wretched thing into the rust bucket, and Esme feared the wheelbarrow would buckle under its weight anyway. But miraculously everything held. They placed the cushions around the owl, tucked in its strange furry feet, and Esme put her jacket loosely over its body. Then Jean took both handles and began to push.

Relieved of his duties as feline paperweight, Hoagy scuttled ahead of them, his tail curling high. At the gates out of the wood, his head flicked from side to side, but the main road was quiet, the hot sun only glimmering down on cars moving up the hill in the distance.

A few passengers peered down at them from the double-decker bus on the main road, but otherwise they got back to Milton Lodge without incident. Londoners were almost medically incurious, Esme thought.

Jean collapsed onto the lawn as Esme fumbled with the key, her fingers sticky with owl blood. She would have that drink now.

'The ridiculous things I find myself doing,' she muttered, but Hoagy was purring gratefully around her legs and when she looked down at him, she was almost certain that he winked.

23

THE CONFESSION

O z led them on through the trees in what he thought was the direction of Sun City. As he did, a new wave of torrential rain began hammering down. He was soon soaked to the skin and barely able to see in front of him. At least anyone looking for them would have a great deal of trouble picking up their trail. But after a while, with the rain obscuring everything, he was forced to admit, if only to himself, that he had no idea which direction they were going in any more.

Luckily, at that moment, the other girl started complaining. 'I'm going to die if I don't eat some of that disgusting black loaf thing immediately.'

Her voice was whining. But to Oz's bemusement, Maggie Blue, who had been quiet ever since the wall of the storm had miraculously collapsed around her, started laughing and did not seem able to stop.

Ida stopped in her tracks, furious, the rain pouring down her face. 'Why are you laughing?'

Maggie shook her head. 'I don't even know. Just the way you said it.'

'Oh my God.' Ida shook her head and rubbed the water out of her eyes. 'This is the end. What are we going to do?'

Maggie sighed, 'I've told you, like, fifty times. I'm going to get you back to the portal and back home.'

'And what about you?'

'I need to find my mum.'

'But you've no idea where she is.'

'Yeah, I know that. . .'

Oz's stomach lurched with guilt. If Maggie knew that her mother had been in the same house as her all along, and that they had left her behind. . . But what could he do? They were lucky to get away as it was; and without Eldrow's inexplicable stubbornness, Maggie would have been dead already. Around him the girls were still bickering.

'Look, if you want to try and find your own way home just . . .'

'As if I can do that.'

'Well shut up then.'

'My parents are going to be so worried. They'll be going crazy.'

'Oh *no*. Will they have to cancel another holiday to the Caribbean? Poor things.'

'They might actually be worried about me. My dad was so freaked out last time.'

'I thought you said he was an idiot,' Maggie responded drily.

'At least he doesn't run off to Canada with some girl who could be his daughter.'

'You sound exactly like your dad.'

'Oh shut up, Maggie.'

'You shut up.'

'I don't know why I came.'

'That makes two of us.'

'I hate this place . . .' The other girl's voice broke a bit. 'I'm scared, Maggie. I really hate it here.'

Maggie stopped and took Ida's hand. A strange energy fizzed between the two girls. When Maggie spoke again, her voice was softer. 'I promise I will get you home. I did it before, didn't I?'

Oz stood quietly beside them. They barely seemed to recall that he existed; they were so focused on each other. Somehow this made him feel even lonelier than he had done when he was really on his own. He wished that the other girl hadn't come and that he had Maggie Blue all to himself.

They came to a slight clearing in the trees where someone before them had built a makeshift shelter: slender twigs threaded through some sturdier branches, all covered with leaves. There was only really room for one person, but it was the best version of cover they had come across in all their tramping, so he forced himself to speak for the first time in many hours. The words felt heavy and difficult to form. 'We should stop here.'

The girls did not object. They were exhausted. Everything was soaking, but they tried to make themselves comfortable with their heads in the sheltered area, at least. He covered them both with the one dry blanket, and they were asleep before he had finished. They had barely spoken a word to him all day. As they slept, Oz watched the bedraggled white crow emerge from Maggie's pocket and perch beside her, keeping watch.

As they slept, he allowed himself to think about his father – the rage that would distort his face when he realised what Oz had done. It gave him a shiver of triumph, but of pure fear, too. He realised that he hoped Eldrow would at least be able to get away. He cared nothing for Almarra or the orbs; they could be crushed in the jaws of the Terrible Ones, as far as he was concerned. He shook his head, shocked by the hardening of the soft heart he had always been teased for . . .

Oz woke, stiff and cold, in that moment of lilac grey just before the white-time. He crawled out of the shelter and looked around: the ground was still very wet but the wind had died down and it was clear and cold. He looked over at the girls who still slept. They were sharing the blanket in their matching black dresses, and Ida's hand rested on Maggie's arm. They were like sisters the way they bickered all day, but then fell asleep so peacefully beside one another. He felt another pang of loneliness but brushed it away.

Oz could hear the trees whispering excitedly amongst themselves. Peering ahead, he noticed an especially old tree a little way through the forest and set off towards it. When he got there, he put his arms around it, his cold cheek pressed to the living bark. At once he felt a deep peace. The trees were still his friends, even if no one else was.

He hoisted himself up nimbly into the lower branches and began to climb. At the top, the thinner branches swayed a little, but he got into their rhythm enough to get a foothold and look out. All around him was an endless flow of trees, but to his astonishment, he saw the peaks of the Magic Mountains in the west, very faint and purplish, but much closer than they should be.

Oz's heart was in his mouth: he had taken them in completely the wrong direction; he was leading them *into* danger, not away from it. His breath came short and his brain scrambled around in panic. What would he tell the girls? He honestly didn't think he could let them know. But the trees had been so dense around him, and the rain so blinding . . .

He descended to the more comfortable lower branches and lay there feeling desperate. The trees were still noisy, chattering to each other. He pressed his ear against the bark and the whispering seemed to get louder. Above him, he saw with surprise that the white crow had left its post beside Maggie and was sitting in a branch just above, staring down at him with its beady eyes. Did it know what he had done? But then the voices took over and for the first time, he could hear strange murmuring words . . . *She is here . . . she is here . . .*

This went on, back and forth between them, until another set of voices seemed to start a little further away: *we will fight . . . we will fight . . . we will fight . . .*

Fight? But trees couldn't fight. Oz lay back in the tree, overwhelmed by all the voices around him. And then a new sharper note from much further away entered the swirl of noise: *the Terrible Ones . . . are coming . . . they are coming . . .*

Oz sat up. He pictured the creatures again, lurking in the gold-tinged dark pool. Almarra had once spoken about the Terrible Ones, the *devroi* she called them. She said they had once been seven lumps of black rock. But now they had come to life, they could hollow you out from the inside until there was only your skin left to fall and shrivel upon the ground. That even the most powerful shifters and moon witches could not withstand them; could not control them, could not fight against them: they were said to eat your soul. Oz shivered; they had to get moving.

He suddenly realised, astonished that the revelation had not struck him at once – he had heard the trees speak . . . he had made out words . . . He wondered if perhaps they could understand him, too. It was worth a try.

He pressed his lips to the bark and said, 'Where is

Maggie Blue's mother?' There was no response. He tried again, 'Is Maggie Blue's mother alive?'

He sat back, feeling foolish. But the noise of the whispering lulled for a moment. And then he heard the voices build around him once again: *she is here. . . she is here. . . we will show you where. . . we will show you where . . .* on and on, almost to a fever pitch. From above, the white crow descended back to the ground in a gentle arc and Oz scrambled down to wake the others.

When he got back, he saw the crow had settled itself beside the sleeping Maggie Blue, but that Ida was awake and had gone into his knapsack and found the black bread. She was gnawing on it like a wild thing. She looked up as he approached.

'Sorry,' she said through a full mouthful, 'I'm starving.'

Oz nodded and watched her, somewhat fascinated. She was an odd mixture of things, this girl.

Ida gulped down a few more mouthfuls then asked, 'Are you all right?'

Oz had not been expecting that. He only said, 'We must be moving again. At once.'

To Oz's surprise, Ida moved towards him and put her arms around his shoulders. 'No, really. Are you OK?'

Oz felt very confused by this. He shook his head in embarrassment. 'All is well.'

'It's just, you remind me of my little brother, Josh. I actually quite miss him.'

'Is Maggie Blue your sister?' Oz blurted out.

Ida looked at him in surprise and laughed. 'Sister? We look kind of different, don't you think?'

'Sisters can be different.'

She giggled. 'I suppose.'

Then suddenly she gave him a big hug. It was the thing he'd been wanting for so long, but now that it came, it shocked him and he pushed her away.

'Sorry,' she said. 'But you're very young to be on your own.'

He couldn't understand why she was mentioning all the things that hurt him. To his relief, Maggie was stirring behind them. She sat up, rubbing her eyes. Immediately the little crow flew to her shoulder and sat looking at them fiercely.

'Do you still know where we're going, Oz?' Maggie asked at once.

'Um, we're not quite where I thought we were.' He sliced off some bread and then passed it to her. Quietly, he said, 'The trees are guiding me.'

But Maggie's voice was louder. 'The trees?'

'I mean, I've spoken to them.'

Behind him, the other girl gave a short brittle laugh. 'Oh God, this is hopeless.'

But Maggie ignored her. 'You can understand them?'

Oz nodded. 'The murmurings I could always hear have turned into words, words I can understand. I think the trees are passing messages between themselves all the time, all through the forest. They're constantly talking. And they know where your mother is; they're going to show me.'

'They are?'

Oz nodded. He said nothing about the Terrible Ones; he would hold that fear to himself. But the fear was in his voice when he said, 'And we have to go *now*.'

The girls looked at each other and got up just as more shards of ice-rain began to fall.

This place was relentless. Maggie had forgotten just how awful it was – the endless trees, the endless cold and rain, the darkness. She felt like she would never be warm again. She longed to see just one shard of sunlight and to stand in it with her eyes closed.

The boy, Oz, kept pressing his ear to the trunks of the ancient trees to listen to what they told him. But what if he was just making it up? Or what if he was leading them into a trap? They knew nothing about him, after all. And Maggie could tell that the boy was more afraid than before. He was on edge, and his eyes darted around all the time, searching for something. But she didn't have any ideas about what else to do, so for now she kept trudging after him.

In her pocket, the white crow was her only source of heat and comfort – a tiny warm patch. Without seeming to communicate with her, she understood that it was in recovery, that it was getting stronger. It soothed her, so quiet and patient by her side.

After a long trudge they came to a large clearing in the trees. There was a wide shallow crater where water had collected. And on one side, a little closer to the trees, there were the sorry remains of a fire, now sodden from the rain.

The ice-rain had finally stopped and above them, the sky was just dipping into the deep blue before darkness fell. Maggie slumped to the ground and Ida fell down beside her and they drank the fresh rainwater from the crater that was only a little muddy.

Oz stayed standing, listening to the trees. He listened intently at the trunk of a very old-looking tree whose gnarled trunk bulged with knots and scars. Then he told her, a little triumphantly, that the trees were whispering to him that her mum was safe and that she was happy.

This made Maggie immediately doubt the whole thing – her mum had never been happy. But, she reasoned, maybe trees had a more general concept of what happiness was. If you were breathing and not being attacked by a predator you were probably classified as pretty cheerful as far as they were concerned.

Every so often the thought kept creeping in – I could go home. I could just get back to the portal and cross. I could be back home with Esme and Hoagy. Hoagy . . . she missed him. How she wished he were here now. One of his sarcastic complaints would be so welcome. She wanted to hug his warm furry body close and hear him purring like a loitering truck. She wondered if he missed her, if Esme did? Or were they relieved to be free of her and all the problems she brought?

For a moment she felt a surge of red . . . why did her mum have to appear? Why had she left the hospital? As usual, everything bad in Maggie's life came back to her. And this was all her fault. *She* was the reason she was traipsing deep into unknown territory to find her on the strength of what some weird little boy said. Maggie sighed – it was better not to think at all really.

Oz lit his lantern and they sat on a dead fallen tree to eat. Afterwards the boy went off into the trees by himself for a while to climb and talk to them. And once he'd gone, Maggie felt more strange energy in the air. Ida kept glancing at her, but at the same time not wanting to meet her eye.

'What is it?' Maggie asked after a while, irritated.

'It's . . . well, it kind of seems stupid to say it now, I mean, here. But . . .' Ida was squirming slightly, and to Maggie's astonishment she saw a very faint blush appear on her cheeks.

Maggie waited, saying nothing, then Ida puffed some air out of her lungs and tried again. Bits of dark leaf were stuck in her thick hair and she had mud on her face. She looked tired and unhappy.

'Look, you know when I came round to see you? And

you hid, and your mum was asleep on the couch and everything?'

Maggie nodded.

'It wasn't about the crow or any of the weird stuff. I was coming over because I wanted to tell you something. I thought I should sort of let you know about . . .'

'What?'

Ida drew a hand over her weary face, but in the lantern-light her eyes sparked a bit. 'About, well, about me and Will.'

Maggie felt like a stone had dropped from her chest into her stomach. *Bang.* She tried to keep her voice sounding normal. 'Will Snowden?'

'We kind of . . . we've kind of been . . . I don't know, kissing a bit.' Ida spat out the last bit with effort and some relief.

Maggie forced a laugh. 'No, seriously?'

'Yeah.'

'So, you're like going out?'

'No, I don't know.'

'For how long?'

'Just a couple of weeks.'

'You kissed him and everything?'

Ida shrugged. 'Yeah.'

'But how are you going to explain it to your *real* friends next term?'

'What do you mean?'

'Well, aren't you going to drop us both when Helena and Daisy come back from holiday?'

'No, no, of course not.'

'Aah, that's so sweet.'

'That's really harsh.' She was silent for a few moments. 'So, do you mind?'

'About what?'

'Me and Will . . . I mean, not that—'

Maggie gulped and it sounded very loud to her, though Ida didn't seem to notice. She felt like she had a lot of phlegm in her mouth that she needed to spit out. And her heart was beating strangely fast. 'Why would I? It seems weird. But it doesn't matter to me.'

'Anyway, who knows if we're even going to see him again, I mean, if we ever get back . . .'

Maggie said nothing and to her relief Ida stopped talking. So it was true . . . and she had probably been round to Will's house without her. Did they talk about her when they were together? Did they say bad things about her? Why hadn't Ida stayed in West Minchen with Will Snowden if they were so happy together, instead of coming here and giving her someone else to be responsible for, someone else to keep safe? If she could have got up and run away, she would have, but there wasn't really anywhere for her to go . . .

24

NEW MASTERS

They had managed to get him back to the house in the nightmarish metal container, which allowed him to feel every bump and dip and jolt as if someone was stabbing him with a knife. When they finally stopped moving, Ulrich used all his remaining strength to shift in the hope it would alleviate his injuries. But it caused him more hideous pain. He cried out, whilst the humans around him reacted hysterically, shrieking and shouting and dancing about. When they had finally recovered themselves, they sort of tipped him onto the floor because their furniture couldn't begin to contain him.

Ulrich lay there in desperate pain. The old lady brought him water into which she dissolved a strange bitter white powder. It alleviated the pain a little, but his wound, the deep wound inflicted upon him by Roda, would not heal. Soon there would be an infection, no matter how many times they cleaned it. Was all his endeavour and loyalty fated to end here? he wondered. In this unclean house, watched over by a battered old cat and a deeply disturbing dead owl that was kept, for reasons unknown, in a dusty glass case above him.

The light was dim and purplish when he awoke. Above him, the one-eyed cat was perched on a piece of furniture. The feline clearly did not trust him and its expression was full of malice. The old woman was examining his wound. She prodded it and he flinched violently, as if he'd been electrocuted. The room swam around him and he couldn't focus. He felt coolness against his forehead but it meant nothing. There were soft voices.

'We should take him to hospital.'

'He's not of this world, dearie. What would we say?'

'We can't let him die.'

But they would, he thought vaguely, and the idea suddenly seemed almost amusing. What would they do with his body? he wondered. Dig a hole in the hard earth outside, a shallow grave. It would be a nobody's departure from this unknown world. But what did it matter after all?

He didn't know how much time had passed, if any, when he heard the voices again, this time more excited. And as he came round, he realised that the two women were trying to sit him up. A searing pain flashed through his abdomen. He cried out and the voices fluttered anxiously around him again. He could barely keep his head up.

Somehow they managed to prop him up again and he

heard a soft voice saying, 'Open your eyes. Can you open them?'

He obeyed and the two faces, one old and pale and one young and dark, blurred and buzzed in his vision. At least he couldn't see that cat, but he knew it would be there somewhere, malingering. A bizarre anger gripped him – if he could do one thing before it was all over, he would crush that feline – and his great hands clenched in impotent aggression.

'Owl-person?' the younger voice was saying. 'Owl-person?'

After a while he realised the voice was talking to him. He tried to focus. 'Yes?'

'He can talk!' the excitable voice announced.

At once, water arrived at his lips and he managed to drink.

'I have found some herbs . . .' It was the old woman again, her voice softer and kinder. 'An old friend gave them to me once when I was bitten by a dog. But she was not your average friend. Some people said she was a witch . . . Maybe . . .'

He could barely follow, nor did he care to. But then his eyes managed to focus on what she held in her hand: it was a jar about half full of tiny green-black pods. Surely he must be hallucinating? He tried to spring up and grab it, but he missed and crashed to the side, howling in pain.

'Oh my goodness,' the old woman's voice said.

The weak hands tried once again to raise him up, but this time they couldn't manage it. From his place on the dusty floor, he managed to say, '. . . a poultice.'

He passed out again until he felt extraordinary coolness and heat concurrently seeping into his wound. He sighed with relief. How this old lady had come by a jar of haemo-globes, one of the rarest plants found in the Strange Plains and one of the most powerful healing herbs, he did not know. But at this point he did not much care either.

He had no idea how much time had passed. But he woke with a start in the darkness and knew for the first time in many days that he was better. He was very shaky and he did not dare try and shift again, but the terrible pain was gone and when he reached for his wound he could tell it was healing over.

The room was utterly silent and still. He could smell dust and old sunlight trapped in here, and he felt a powerful urge to go outside. He heaved himself to standing and went over to the door. It was locked but the structure was weak and his powerful hands easily forced it – he had not lost all his strength it seemed. He stepped out into the high cool night and breathed in the air with relief.

The large wide garden spread out before him – he knew it well, having perched in the great oak for so many moons, watching. But he needed to get some real movement going. So he edged round the side of the house and down the drive until he came to the road beyond on which, occasionally, one of the terrifying speeding vehicles, lights blazing, rushed past. Very slowly, he began to walk.

Apart from the loud but fleeting noise of each vehicle, the hard roads were quiet and still. He turned into a narrower street. Here there was a proliferation of trees, flowers closed for the night and other plants all carefully encased in separate adjoining plots. Most of the windows were dark, but those that weren't emitted a rich yellow glow, both welcoming and intent upon shutting out the world.

Ulrich felt drawn to this strict and regular division of territory. Some of the houses were in total darkness and appeared to be uninhabited. It struck him that he could easily force his way into one and remain there undiscovered. He was sizing up a large double-fronted building with an empty driveway when he suddenly began to feel weak once more.

He leant against a low wall and took some deep painful breaths. And then his slightly numbed senses twitched and he knew he was not alone, and hadn't been for the entirety of this walk. He looked round; a shadow moved. He grimaced – he had almost forgotten.

Perhaps the old mog realised subterfuge was no longer required, because a moment later it appeared from behind a large bush and sat obnoxiously in the middle of the road, staring him down and making no further attempt to conceal itself. Ulrich had had enough. He gathered up his strength and strode right towards the ancient cat and as he got closer, he raised his fist. But the one-eyed one did not flinch. One warrior recognised another and the huge man paused.

His huge fist unclenched. 'Why do you watch me all the time?' he asked gruffly.

The cat's eye blinked once, and then it said, 'Because I don't trust you. Where is Maggie Blue?'

Always the girl. 'I don't know.'

The cat hissed and spat. 'What has happened to her?'

'And why should you care, cat?' Ulrich asked.

'That is no concern of yours. But I saw you take her, I was there that night. You took her against her will. You have been nursed back to health, though I would person-ally have let you die, but Maggie is still gone.'

Ulrich relented a little – he saw the logic there. 'I don't know where she is now. But I can tell you the last time I saw her.'

'She was alive?'

He nodded. 'She was.'

'And was she in immediate danger?'

Ulrich thought of the wild fight just outside the portal but he shook his head. 'I don't think so,' he lied.

The cat's features softened with relief and Ulrich felt an unexpected pang. The girl was loved; someone cared for her. He felt ludicrously alone, but warriors should be alone, they were meant to be so. His shoulders dropped and the fighter's stance dropped with them. He turned and started walking again, and the cat simply followed.

When he woke up the next morning, all three of them were there – the old lady, the girl and the cat. What a bizarre tribe, he thought, as he eased himself up to sitting. They all stared at him expectantly.

'That cat has told me that you want to know about Maggie Blue.'

The woman and girl looked at each other in amazement.

'You can talk to the cat?' the girl said, almost laughing.

'You can't?' Ulrich said.

'Oh no, dearie.' The old lady smiled indulgently. 'Hoagy's a cat, you see.'

'And?'

There was loud purring and Ulrich glared down at Hoagy, who smiled at him smugly and said, 'But they do want to know what happened to Maggie. What you told me last night.'

Ulrich looked back at the astonished faces of the humans. One constantly had to remind oneself of how simple and stupid they were.

'So you know about Maggie?' the old lady asked eagerly.

Ulrich studied her properly for the first time. She was wearing a curious turquoise gown with garish flowers sewn on it, and her two-tone hair was held up with some sort of stick.

'I saw her in the other world,' he said.

'You *took* her there,' hissed the cat. 'You abducted her.'

Ulrich ignored this.

'What is she doing there?' the woman asked.

'The Fathers want her.'

'The Fathers?'

'The rulers of the Island.' They looked blank. 'My world.'

'Will they let her go afterwards?'

'I hope so.'

The brown furry body suddenly leapt at him and its claws dug into his skin and tried to rip it. 'Liar! Liar!'

'Hoagy! What on earth . . . ?' the old lady cried out, and tried to grab the cat.

But there was no need. Ulrich swiped the cat away so that it flew across the room, slammed into a glass cabinet and slid onto the moth-eaten carpet. But it still managed to mewl out weakly, 'Tell the truth.'

There was a pause in the general hysteria while Esme made 'tea', a brown hot steaming liquid into which animal's milk was then poured. It was quite disgusting but the others seemed to relish it. There were also some pale hard biscuits to eat that the lady identified as shortbread, which were far more interesting. He ate about five of these. Then the old lady adjusted her spectacles and folded her arms; the young woman had no glasses, but she folded her arms in just the same way. Ulrich understood what the body language meant – resistance was futile.

'What *are* you?' the tall girl asked after a long silence. 'I'm Jean, by the way. And this is Esme. I mean, sorry if that question seems a bit rude, but I think it's kind of fair. You have gone from an owl into a man, like, that is fairly cool. But odd, if you don't mind me saying so.'

Ulrich shook his head, feeling bemused. Why did these people talk so much? 'I am a shifter – a warrior shifter. You understand?'

'A warrior?'

'Yes. It is my job to protect the Great O. Or, well, it was.'

'Who's the Great O?' the old lady called Esme cut in.

The girl's leg was bouncing up and down in a manner Ulrich found intolerable and the cat was purring and shooting him daggers concurrently. He felt exhausted by the whole thing, and all he wanted to do was sleep and forget about everything. But he ploughed on.

'The Great O is the protector of nature. She creates harmony and balance in our world. Or, well, she used to. Warrior shifters are born to protect her. We are born, live and die for her. All other shifters are banished from the Magic Mountains at birth. They are lowly, useless creatures. Many of them have lowered themselves to being scouts and spies for the Islanders, and they cross through the portals to bring them whatever their greed desires.'

The purple girl was frowning. 'Well what else are they supposed to do? They get banished from the good place. Are they just supposed to die or something?'

Ulrich started at her. He opened his mouth but nothing came out. He had never thought of it quite like that.

'What's a shifter, dearie?' the old woman asked. She was peering at him from behind very large glasses, her face a crumple of confusion. There was a lot of dust in this room and it was a horrible mess, with papers, books and empty cups everywhere. Ulrich resisted the urge to leap up and punch a hole in the nearest wall and took a breath.

'A shape-shifter. We can alter our form – become animal or human, and at times of terrible danger, an object. We can enter and control other minds, and some can destroy other minds. The Children, a very rare form whose animal is actually an orb of light . . . they can end you at will. But that is unusual.'

'So you can enter my mind?' Jean asked, wide-eyed.

'Of course.'

'But . . . what? That is so creepy. So, so creepy.'

'My, my . . . so you can tell what we're thinking, can you?' Esme shook her head in disbelief. 'So could you tell what Maggie was thinking the last time you saw her?'

'No. She has the ability to block those who try and enter her mind. It's because—'

Suddenly the cat started up with a frightful mewling and began ripping at the material on the sofa arm with his claws. Then he repeatedly rammed his head against the old lady's arm.

She stroked his head and said soothingly, 'Yes, my

darling, I see.' She looked back at Ulrich. 'Where is Maggie Blue and how do we get her home?'

'The last time I saw her she was by the portal near Sun City. I'm not sure where she is now.'

'So we just go back there and get her?' Jean offered.

'I can't.'

'Why not?'

'Because the Great O wants her – she needs her.'

'But why?'

'We don't know; we only obey the Great O. You must be aware that Maggie Blue is not a normal child?'

They two humans looked at each other and surprised him by laughing. 'Well, yes, we had rather gathered that, dearie,' Esme said. 'But I still don't see why you can't just go and get her back.'

'She is part-shifter – she doesn't appear to change between forms but she has some of our mental powers and she can cross between worlds. She was born in this world, but she is from our world.'

'I'm sorry, dearie, that's just not true. I mean her mother—'

'Is an Islander,' Ulrich interrupted. 'She is from our world, too. And Maggie's father is a shifter.' He wrinkled his nose in instinctive disgust; he did not want to consider that too closely. 'Such relations are strictly forbidden. As far as is known, or as far as I have ever known, Maggie Blue is the only part-shifter ever to have been born, or at least to have been allowed to survive.'

Esme was still as a statue, lost in thought. 'My word, Cynthia from another world, is it?' She laughed again and this time it was tinged with hysteria. 'I suppose it does make a funny kind of sense. Lion could never make head nor tail of her. But then, he is an idiot.' She froze, though her eyes kept moving restlessly about in her head. Then she turned to him once more. 'But Maggie didn't want to go back. She was terrified of that place. Did you force her to go back?'

'Those were our orders,' he said dully.

'But why does this Great O thing want her? Why does it need Maggie? What could this thing possibly want with a mere girl?'

Ulrich hesitated and the cat began to tear at the grimy old sofa fabric again. His one eye was fixed upon him.

The girl was frowning hard, 'Wait, is Maggie . . . ? Is she . . . ? I mean, is Maggie some sort of sacrifice?'

Ulrich hesitated, but there was little point in dissembling any more. 'We wondered if that was her role, but we do not know. We only obey the Great O; we do not question her.'

'A sacrifice?!' Esme had leapt from her chair and short-bread crumbs had fallen everywhere. 'This mother nature thing is going to kill her?'

Ulrich shrugged. 'I truly do not know. I never did.'

This information hung in the air like poisonous spores and everyone was slowly breathing them in. Finally the cat spoke, though Ulrich now assumed the humans could only hear mewlings or purrs.

'You will help us find her.'

'What did Hoagy say?' Esme asked.

'He says I must help you find her.'

'And so you must,' Esme retorted. 'It's the least you can do. You kidnapped her, dearie. She's had a difficult life, things were just getting better and you ruined it all again. You're darn right you're helping us bring her home.'

Ulrich tried to say something, but the old lady held up her hand with surprising imperiousness. 'Not another word. Your masters have changed; you obey us from now on.'

PART THREE

25

A NEW BLACK

25

A NEW PLACE

They emerged from the trees into a wide clearing with a brownish-red mountain rising in the distance. Beside the pebbly ground was another huge expanse of water. But it wasn't grey and forbidding. It shimmered in the white-time light, and beyond it, pink cliffs the colour of rose quartz rose up and were reflected back in the water.

'Where are we?' Maggie asked.

Oz shook his head. 'I don't know, but the trees say your mother is here.' *Hopefully without my father*, he added silently in his head.

Maggie went to the water's edge, washed her hands and face and drank – the water was cold and pure. She looked back at Ida and Oz. They had moved slightly so that they could rest against a large grey-pink rock. She stared at the boy, at his matted jet-black hair and his dirty face. Could he really hear the trees talking? Or was he a little touched from the loneliness she felt in him – she didn't really think her mum was here.

She felt the white crow move in her pocket. It had not moved for a long time but now, first its head and then its brilliant-white body appeared. Without a glance at her, it took off and flew straight towards the pink cliffs.

'Hey!' Maggie called after it.

But the bird ignored her and flew up to the very top of the cliff face where it perched, transformed into a small white spot.

She went back over to the others. 'I'll take a look around.' Oz's mouth opened, so she quickly added, 'You both stay here. I won't be long.'

Ida nodded vaguely and the boy's mouth shut again, so Maggie started walking round the edge of the lake before anyone could object. She could feel the white crow pulling at her; it wanted to show her something. As she got closer, Maggie realised it might be possible to climb up the cliff face itself – large uneven steps had formed in the rock.

It was a tiring but not difficult climb, and before long Maggie was heaving herself onto a small plateau just below the cliff top. The bird was waiting for her and watched impassively as she lay back, panting. But as soon as she'd recovered, it turned and flew into a small cave set into the rock that darkened from pink to purple.

Maggie followed it inside. A few feet back from the opening she found the crow sitting patiently beside the body of Cynthia Brown. Maggie could see her chest rising and falling – her mum was fast asleep beside the remnants of a small fire.

A feeling of intense relief flooded over her . . . Her mum was safe, nothing bad had happened, everything might still be OK. She edged closer. Even in the dim light, she could see that her mum was looking better than she had in West Minchen: there was colour in her cheeks and her face looked less drawn.

This was not quite what she had expected. Maggie had kind of imagined her mum grabbing her and holding her close, thanking her through tears for coming to the rescue. But at that moment she didn't look like she was in need of much help. Maggie felt the familiar red begin to pulse through her as she fought back the urge to shake her mum awake, to disturb her peace. She felt childish and unkind, but she couldn't help it.

She went back outside and sat with her legs hanging over the rocky ledge. She looked out over the Dark World, from the small figures of Ida and Oz beside the lake, to the forest stretching away like a dark blanket beyond them. She knew she shouldn't hesitate: she should wake her mum and begin the long journey back to the portal. But she did not have the energy . . . or the will.

'Maggie?'

Her mum was standing behind her. She had finally dumped the grubby and tattered pink dressing gown she'd been wearing for the last two years, and had opted for a thick white robe that made it look like she'd joined a cult. She was staring at Maggie in astonishment.

'What are you doing here?'

The question threw Maggie for a moment. She'd thought it was obvious, but maybe not. 'I came here to find you.'

'We were hoping you would have crossed back.'

'We?'

'Myself and Roda.'

'The heron?' For a moment Maggie didn't understand, but then, of course, Cynthia couldn't have made it here alone.

'He rescued me.'

'From where?'

'I don't really know. It was a big house by a lake.'

'You were at the house?' Maggie exclaimed. She looked down at Oz and again she wondered about him. But she only said, 'No one told me.'

'I don't really remember anything. They kept me unconscious somehow. I just saw a glimpse of the place as we flew away – I've never seen it before. And then we came here.'

'Where is Roda now?'

'He's gone to get food and to see what is happening . . . to see if we are safe here.'

Maggie closed her eyes for a moment and took a deep breath. 'OK, look, we need to get back to the portal in the woods. It might be a long journey, but if we can get back there, I can get us all home.'

To her utter astonishment, her mum shook her head. 'I'm not leaving.'

'What?'

Her mum smiled slightly. 'I tried to tell you before, but you didn't want to hear it. This is my home . . . I am from this world.'

Everything seemed to stop except for her pounding heartbeat that hammered wildly in her ears. The white crow flew up to Maggie's shoulder and the little dig of its claws kept her steady. She turned away from Cynthia and stared back out at the Dark World.

'I admit, I wondered if you had come here when you disappeared last year. And now Roda has told me all about you: that you can cross, that you have certain powers – that you are special.'

'Not special enough,' Maggie muttered, but Cynthia did not hear.

'This is what I was trying to tell you at Esme's. I was born here into one of the seven great families. But something happened . . . and I had to leave.'

A wave of emotion that Maggie could neither recognise nor understand broke through her painfully and rose up into her throat so that, for a moment, she found it hard to breathe. She stared at a distant point on the horizon, stared at it like her eyes could bore into it. Then she grabbed a bit of skin on her inner forearm and pinched it as hard as she could until she felt enough pain to keep it together.

'I so appreciate . . . It's so extraordinary that you . . .' Cynthia broke off again, unable to continue.

She never had been able to say thank you, Maggie thought with bitterness.

'I mean, it's just I feel so much better here. Roda has told me that this world is dying, and I can see it, I can feel it. But for the first time in nearly fourteen years, I don't feel afraid – I don't feel like I'm going mad. I don't know how else to explain it to you. But when you've felt like I have . . . well, I can't leave, not yet anyway.'

Maggie felt sharp hysteria rising in her. 'Well, I'm certainly glad I came then.'

The white crow's claws dug in harder. At the same time, a flash of knowledge burst into Maggie's brain: something about the way the heron had stared at her so intently all those months ago in the moon witches' hut, something about why a cold warrior shifter would care so much about a human like Cynthia Brown that it would go to the trouble of rescuing and bringing her here . . . something about why Lion barely bothered to keep in touch . . . Her voice was flat and unfamiliar when she spoke. 'Is Roda my dad?'

She turned back; her mum looked white. Clearly she hadn't meant to tell her everything. 'Maggie . . . he didn't know . . . he thought I was dead. Until a few days ago, he thought we were both dead. Dead years ago . . .'

The hysterics bubbled back up. 'So, let me get this

236

straight, my dad's a heron and you're happy to stay here? Good, no, really, that's good to know.'

Suddenly Maggie couldn't stop laughing; she bent double and weird heaves of laughter were coming out of her mouth and her whole body trembled. She thought she was going to be sick, but she couldn't stop.

Behind her, Cynthia Brown said and did nothing. She did not reach out to her, hug her or squeeze her hand – she froze, as she had always done at the sight of any emotion. Only the presence of the white crow anchored Maggie to the ground and stopped her from floating off and disappearing altogether like vapour in the air.

'Maggie?'

For a millisecond, she thought her mum was actually talking to her. But the delusion soon passed. It was only little Oz and he was smiling. But then he saw the tear stains on her cheeks and immediately he looked worried. 'Are you all right?'

Maggie wiped them away, recovering herself. 'I'm fine.'

He hauled himself up onto the ledge close beside her and was followed by a fairly angry looking Ida. When they saw Cynthia standing there, they both just stared dumbly.

'This is my mum: we've found her! But as it turns out, she loves the climate here, so we really needn't have bothered risking everything to come and save her,' Maggie explained, then burst out laughing again and bent double, her stomach muscles were hurting so much.

Ida and Oz looked horrified and slightly afraid of her weird laughter.

'Is there anyone else here?' Oz asked peering into the cave.

Maggie shook her head. But her mum smiled at them and beckoned them into the cave. 'Why don't you come in and rest for a bit? You look tired.'

And they followed like lambs. Cynthia Brown seemed to have developed some basic social skills since she had been in the Dark World, which was nice. For a moment the hysteria threatened again, but suddenly Maggie shivered. The light was starting to drain away; the temperature was dropping rapidly. She had no idea what to do now.

And then she listened as Oz began talking to her mum in the cave, more than Maggie had ever heard him talk before. He told her about their escape, how everyone had been under a sleeping spell, how Maggie made the storm disappear, how the trees had led them here.

'The trees?'

Oz tried to explain but no one was listening; a collective fatigue gripped them. As the boy helped Cynthia to relight the fire, Maggie went into the cave and sat beside Ida who had not spoken at all. Maggie squeezed her hand and after a moment, Ida squeezed back.

'Does my hair look really bad?' Ida asked.

Maggie looked at her. There were leaves wedged into the thick curls, her face was dirty and she had bruises and cuts all over her hands and her legs. 'It kind of needs a brush,' Maggie offered.

They shared out the last of their food and then exhaustion overwhelmed them. Maggie had just enough time to arrange a blanket and fall down beside Ida, and she was out.

26

THE KNIFE

Maggie woke with a start. For a moment she had no idea where she was. But then her eyes grew accustomed to the darkness and she made out the three sleeping bodies beside her and the umber glow of a dying fire. It was freezing – perhaps that was what had woken her? She closed her eyes and tried to ignore the chill, but something kept nagging her awake. Eventually she sat up and crawled out of the cave.

Hanging low over the lake was a full and beautiful moon, so heavy that it looked as if it might drop into the water and disappear. She remembered how hard she'd had to yank Hoagy's tail to get him to stop staring at it when they were in the Dark World together, and how he'd lashed out and told her never to touch his sacred tail again. She smiled for a moment . . . she missed him. If only he could be here now, just to snuggle close to her, just to tell her she was an idiot.

Instead she felt a peck on her arm. Startled, Maggie turned and saw the white crow beside her. Its pure white body reflected the moonlight and it glowed like a lantern. Maybe she was losing it, but these days it felt as if this crow was the only one who understood her at all, except maybe Hoagy. But he was so far away at this moment, and it felt so lonely being the only one awake. The bird flew up to her shoulder and she smiled as once again she felt its claws dig gently into her skin.

But then the crow began to peck at her, over and over with its small sharp beak.

'Hey, hey, get off,' Maggie hissed and swiped it away. 'What is it?' The crow let out a low cawing and she saw, rising up out of the dark forest to the east, a haze of kaleidoscopic colours that shimmered and swayed above the treetops. Maggie gasped; she knew what those colours meant. It was a full moon, when the moon witches believed they could see the future, and they were fairly close by.

The crow took off and flew down to the water's edge. It wanted her to go with it into the forest. But why? The last time they'd met, the witches had tried to kill her. But the glowing white bird began cawing loudly, making a weird regurgitating movement as it did so. This bird was the only thing she trusted right now . . . there must be a good reason it wanted her to follow. She looked back at the humped shadows of the sleepers – no one else seemed to need her much anyway.

241

At the water's edge, Maggie felt an extra blast of cold and shivered into her thick dress. She walked towards the dense forest and when she got under its canopy, she had the eerie sense that the trees were watching her. She stood and listened for a moment. For the first time she understood Oz's bizarre idea that they were talking to each other. There was a sort of hushed whispering noise. But the white crow did not want her to stop. It glowed like a lantern in front of her, and she kept after it like a sleepwalker.

After a few minutes of walking on through the trees, swirling colours suddenly reared up out of the dark and Maggie dropped to the ground, pressing herself into the cold wet leaves. There was the strange hissing noise that she remembered from last time, and in a small clearing the fierce moonlight shone onto a sombre gathering of hooded moon witches.

There were about ten of them, standing in a circle, their lanterns wedged into the earth just behind them so that they seemed to be surrounded by fire. In the centre, the ancient, with his long flowing white hair, lay naked on the ground. Two witches pressed and massaged his feet with their spindly bony fingers. The moonlight bounced off the ancient's grotesque transparent skin and the colours crackled and danced in the air above him.

But Maggie didn't think the ancient was the one she had seen before . . . he looked younger and stronger. As before, the attendant witches let his feet drop and he groaned as the colours abruptly vanished. All that was left was their juddering echo in the darkness. But as it cleared, Maggie saw his violet eyes blazing right at her, as if he could see her lying there in the dirt.

Another witch went forward to assist him with his robe and then helped him stand up. The others had gathered their lanterns and moved closer to him, expectantly, so that the light flickered malevolently over his ghoulish face. Gradually the strength seemed to return to his frail body and he stood up straighter. His voice when he spoke was like a song, strong, lulling and flowing.

'I have seen it again; nothing has changed; I have seen what my forbear could not.' His eyes glittered with excitement. 'The girl brings the darkness. But she is a nothing, a conduit, a bridge between worlds. The moon still insists that it is the Great O who wants to destroy us!'

Shrieks and howls of consternation broke spontaneously from the witches around him. But he held up his hideous transparent hands and the noise stopped.

Then one lone witch asked, 'But why?'

The ancient's head snapped round to the speaker. 'She is heart-broken, in pain, weak. But her determination is steely – I feel that. And I feel her very close by, *very* close. She has returned to our world: that is certain. And so has the girl. But since we cannot live in harmony, the Great O will destroy everything, destroy the world she loves rather than let the Fathers destroy it for her. And the destruction will be terrible; it will be a terrible punishment.'

243

'So we must fight the Fathers?' another asked.

The ancient nodded. 'Of course, if we can defeat them there is a chance. But we must still find and destroy the girl. She is intertwined in the fate of our world, and her destruction may change things yet. Everything hangs in the balance.'

Lying there, covered in leaves and mud, her finger-nails full of soil, Maggie's heart was beating like crazy. Fascinating as it was, she didn't fancy sticking around to hear any more of the ancient's grizzly plans for her future. She began to crawl away as silently and as quickly as she could, back the way she had come.

When she thought she'd got far enough away, she dared to stop and look back. To her intense relief, the clearing had vanished, and all was quiet and dark once again. Even the trees had stopped whispering. But suddenly the white crow swooped down overhead, screeching wildly. It was a warning. Maggie dragged herself up and started to run but she had barely covered any ground before the moon witches floated down from the trees and landed all around her, their black cloaks opening briefly like dark flowers in bloom.

They surrounded her in a small circle, silent and still as the lantern flames flickered over their hooded faces. Maggie began to shake. She did not want to feel their bony hands around her neck. And she felt a flash of deep anger at the crow for bringing her here . . . perhaps it had meant to betray her all along. Around her, she heard the trees start to whisper again . . . if she didn't make it, perhaps they would tell little Oz what had happened to her.

No one moved for a minute or so, then the circle parted and the ancient stepped towards her, his violet eyes burning. Maggie felt terror and adrenaline bubbling up inside her as every hooded head turned to him reverentially. And in that split second, Maggie took her chance. She span round and dived through the dark bodies behind her.

She crashed through the trees, but the moon witches were like panthers. In a few seconds they would catch her. Around her, the air was filled with awful noise: the shrieks and howls of the witches and something else too – a grinding, a rumbling. And her brain was getting confused: every time she tried to dodge past a tree, she misjudged the angle and nearly crashed into it.

Eventually she completely mistimed it, smashed into one of the ancient trunks and fell back, screaming in pain. She lay on the ground, her head throbbing, waiting for the bodies to drop onto her, to grip onto her. But nothing happened. If anything, the howls of the moon witches seemed fainter, or maybe she was fainting? Her head throbbed painfully. But still nothing happened.

After a long while she sat up, still feeling dizzy, and found herself right in the middle of a tight circle of trees. It was unnatural somehow, like an optical illusion. 'Did I get away?' she mumbled to no one in particular.

The white crow flew to her shoulder, illuminating the scene, and Maggie let out a deep sigh of relief. But then she heard a slight rustling and a shadow dropped out of the trees.

They were very close, only a few feet away from each other. Maggie could hear its ragged breath, and see a pulse throbbing violently in one thin transparent wrist.

Instinctively, she held up her hands. 'Please, please don't hurt me.'

She couldn't tell if the witch was male or female, but its voice was high and soft when it spoke. 'Every full moon since you came to our land, the ancient has seen that you are fated to destroy us.'

'But how could I do that, even if I wanted to?'

The creature shook its head. 'It doesn't matter how or even why. All we know is that we cannot destroy the Great O, but we can destroy you.' There was no malice in the voice.

Maggie backed away, then turned and tried to run, but the thing was upon her at once. It knocked her to the ground and she felt the strong bony hands clench around her neck. The pain was awful, mind-bending, and she tried to kick and hit out. But the pressure only grew – she was choking, all the strength was draining from her body.

Suddenly a blinding light seared through the darkness. The witch screamed and fell back, writhing on the ground in terrible pain. Great gusts of breath hammered in and out of Maggie's chest and she sat up, spluttering and coughing.

She was shaking violently. In the dazzling light she could just make out the crow hovering above the witch, who seemed pinned to the ground. But its light was already fading slightly. She needed to go right now.

Somehow she managed to get to her feet and as she did, she felt something: a forgotten object in the pocket of her itchy and now filthy dress. She drew it out and stared at the leather parcel in her shaking hands. Inside she found the knife; she stared at it dumbly, mesmerised by the dull glint.

At that moment, she heard the crow fall to the ground. The light from its quivering body had weakened enough that the moon witch could sit up, though its eyes still streamed with tears. It took a moment for its vision to return, but then it locked onto Maggie and saw the blade in her hand.

It flitted with great speed up a tree and she could hear it moving in the canopy. Maggie ran, waving the dagger around her head to try and stop the witch attacking from above. All she could hear was her own breath, crushing painfully in her bruised lungs. Just when she needed to move, fatigue swamped her limbs and despite her fear she wasn't sure she could keep going. Her chest was burning.

The white crow had recovered enough to fly ahead of her, screeching and calling to her, trying to get her back to safety. But after a while Maggie had to stop. Her neck felt badly bruised and sore. She clutched her sides and bent at the waist, trying to get her breath back.

When she'd finally stopped gasping, she realised there was total silence, but the quietude was full of menace. She stood stock-still for long excruciating moments, listening for any sound. Then there came a tiny rustle right above her. Her head flipped back and she saw purple eyes staring down. With a wild banshee-like cry the witch launched itself at her. Maggie managed to take a tiny step backwards, and as the witch fell, she slashed wildly at its falling shadow.

The witch screamed, an awful desolate sound, and fell in a heap on the ground beside her. Maggie scrambled away, horrified. By the crow's faint glow, she could see a pool of thick blood seeping into the forest floor like red mercury. The crumpled-up body of the witch moaned and looked up at her.

'I'm sorry,' Maggie whispered, still keeping her distance. But the witch's eyes lolled back in its head and she wasn't sure if it heard or understood. Suddenly, with an awful groan, it threw off its cloak and lay naked for a few moments, wriggling like a fish gasping for air, transparent and horrible. Then it tucked itself up into a tiny ball and rolled away into the dark forest.

Maggie fell back in exhaustion and shock. She wasn't sure how long she stayed there but eventually she wiped the dagger carefully on the ground and tucked it back into her pocket. The black cloak lay discarded on the ground, blood-stained but otherwise intact. Maggie threw it around her, thinking it could help her stay out of sight. Then finding her horror and fear had given her one last burst of energy, she ran.

She still hadn't made it to the lake when she had to stop again. She leant against a tree and a feeling of profound exhaustion and hopelessness washed over her. The witch's blood had seeped all over the earth, staining it for ever. The smell of skin and metallic blood filled her nostrils and she retched, then fell to the ground.

Moments later, the white crow landed in her lap. It too was exhausted. Maggie stroked its tiny head and sighed deeply. Gradually and almost imperceptibly, a white haze grew around them. It seeped into her tired mind and after a while Maggie felt peaceful, something she had not felt for a long time.

In the distance she could hear vague shrieks, and the trees were whispering again. But it was all a long way away and of no real importance. She breathed more easily and the bruising around her neck stopped hurting so much. A bubble of white light surrounded them.

She looked down at the strange little bird in her lap and it twisted its neck round to look up at her. Energy and knowledge passed between them. And suddenly, with a weird click somewhere in her brain, when a piece of knowledge rose up to her so certainly, Maggie understood, she felt it. The white crow had wanted her to witness the full moon ritual because it needed her to understand something – the moon witches' visions were true: she *was* here to destroy this world.

Maggie laughed suddenly. Warm invisible waves radiated from the white bird into Maggie and she knew something else too: the crow *was* the ouroboros ring. And far more than that, they were both the Great O: she had been with her all along in different forms – object and now animal. Perhaps later she would become a human?

It was just as Dot had told her when she had refused to listen, when she had fought against the idea. She *was* special . . . she *was* from two worlds. The Great O had chosen her; she was with her and she would not let her go. And, at that moment, Maggie did not want it to.

The energy kept flowing between them – the invisible thread vibrating and shimmering. The Great O was so powerful, and yet Maggie could feel her vulnerability. She needed her help. Maggie would take the Great O back to the Magic Mountains, and there she would destroy this godforsaken world where greed and brutality had disfigured everything. Together they would put this world out of its misery; together they would stem the Fathers' denial of reality by inflicting a reality upon them they could no longer ignore. This was Maggie's only purpose and her only task. She looked down at the quivering white crow and felt deeply at peace. For the very first time in Maggie's whole life, everything made sense.

27

SHE'S BEHIND YOU

It was no exaggeration to say that when Oz woke up on the hard floor of the cave, and realised Maggie Blue had disappeared, he descended into a state of total panic. He looked out of the cave but no one was there. And when he scrambled down the cliff she was not to be found by the lake either. So he made straight for the forest and climbed up into the most ancient tree he could find. When he'd calmed down enough to ask the murmuring trees if they knew where Maggie Blue had gone, it was almost as if they were laughing at him . . . *She's behind you . . . she's behind you . . . she is safe . . .*

Oz heaved a huge sigh of relief and wondered what he'd been most afraid of: some harm befalling Maggie or the idea that she had left him willingly, looked down at his sleeping body and walked away. The idea of her leaving him terrified him – so much for being brave.

He shimmied back down to the ground, and just as the

trees promised, he found her close by, leaning against a tree with her eyes closed, her head lolling to one side. The white crow was resting in her lap. But as soon as he approached, its beady eyes fixed onto him and did not let him go.

Then Oz saw the blood. There was a smear of it on Maggie's cheek and, as he drew nearer still, he realised that the strange black cloak she wore around her shoulders was covered in it too. The trees sang around him – they sounded jubilant – but Oz was filled with dread. Something had happened to Maggie Blue . . . something about her had changed. But what? He approached and very gently, so as not to wake her, rubbed the blood off her face.

Now they were sitting by the lake and the white crow was delicately drinking from the shallows at the water's edge. The beatific reverie Maggie had been in when he'd found her was over, and she was pale and shivery beside him. It was like she had seen a ghost . . . she looked haunted. And for some reason, he could not persuade her to take off the soiled bloodied cloak. Its metallic stench filled his nostrils and made him feel sick.

She'd barely said a word since he had found her, so he tried again. 'What happened, Maggie?'

This time he caught her attention and she finally seemed to see him. 'I killed someone, Oz . . . or something. With the knife . . . remember the knife you gave me?'

He'd never for a minute thought . . . he caught his breath. 'Who did you kill?'

'A moon witch. Or, at least, I think I killed it. There was a lot of blood . . .' Her voice trembled and she stopped and turned to him. 'It was self-defence. It was going to kill me.'

'But why did you go to the forest? Why didn't you wake me?'

Maggie smiled wanly and nodded at the crow. 'It wanted me to. It was a full moon and the witches were out and about having their prophecies about me . . . you know, the usual.' She laughed, but it was a harsh disembodied sound. 'The white crow thought I should hear what they were saying about me.'

Oz frowned. 'Why?'

'Because it turns out that what they're saying is true.' She shook her head. 'It's nothing for you to worry about, little Oz.'

She turned away to stare out over the lake again and he watched her. It was as if she wasn't really with him any more . . . she was somewhere else, thinking about things she thought he couldn't understand, but he was sure that he could, if only she would tell him what was going on.

But then she surprised him by suddenly turning and looking at him intently. 'Why didn't you tell me my mum was in that house all along? Did you know?' Her voice was hard.

The blood rushed to Oz's face. He nodded. 'Almarra and Eldrow were told to kill you and if they did not, the Terrible Ones were coming for you – there was no time.'

'Kill me?' She laughed again in the same hollow way. 'They'll have to join the queue.'

'It's not funny, Maggie. The Terrible Ones . . . I don't know what they can do exactly, but they frighten me.'

Maggie frowned at him suddenly. 'Why do you care? I mean, aren't you from their side?' Her eyes narrowed. 'Me and Ida never believed all that stuff about you being kidnapped from Sun City.'

'But I was. They came and took me. They took me from Suri, my nurse, she—' Suddenly and without warning all his defences broke and he was trying to speak through tears. 'I don't know . . . I mean she must be . . . I miss her . . .'

'Oh, Oz. I'm sorry.'

She hugged him close and he cried his eyes out against the horrible blood-stained cloak. But it was a relief to let it all go, as if the tight knot inside him had finally been loosened. When he'd recovered a little, he hung his head and could not look her in the eye.

'I wanted to be brave,' he mumbled.

Maggie Blue laughed but at least she sounded more like herself. 'How old are you?'

Oz shook his head. 'I'm not sure any more. A hundred moons, last time anyone counted.'

She shrugged. 'I don't know what that means, but I can tell you're younger than me.' She took his hand. 'You *are* brave. I've seen you. We'd never have made it here if you hadn't helped us. Without you, the Terrible Ones would have taken me already, wouldn't they? Just like you said.'

She let his hand fall and looked out across the water again. 'And I've been thinking, last night, I could hear the trees talking, not words or anything, but they were murmuring – I heard it.'

Oz was filled with excitement. 'You can hear them too? I thought no one believed me.'

'But something else . . . it was like they were helping me.'

'What do you mean?'

'I can't explain it. I know it's impossible: trees don't move. But there were at least ten moon witches on my tail. You know how fast they move through the trees? I should have had no chance, but somehow I got away. I bumped against one of the trunks and when I came to, the trees were in this tight circle around me that didn't look natural. It was weird. In the end, only one witch got through . . . that's why I had to . . .'

Oz was filled with awe. 'If the trees are helping you, you must be very important.'

But Maggie shook her head. 'I'm not important at all. I wish I was.'

He wanted to say, but you are, you're everything to me. But instead, without planning it, he found himself confessing.

'Maggie?'

'Yes?'

'There is one thing I haven't told you.'

She smiled again. 'What's that?'

'About Eldrow . . . He's . . . he's my father. I only found out once they'd taken me to the house. I mean, that's what he told me. I don't even know if it's true.'

The big grey eyes had become hard again. 'You're Eldrow's son?'

He nodded. 'I think so.'

'You think so?'

'I don't really know him. He was violent and strange in the house, but then when your mother arrived, he changed completely. He carried her down to the lower floor in his arms and never left her side.'

Maggie frowned. 'That is odd.' She was still looking at him strangely. 'He tried to kill me once.'

Oz bowed his head; he felt a deep shame. 'I'm sorry.'

Above them, at the top of the cliff, Maggie Blue's mother and Ida suddenly appeared. They were waving their hands at them and shouting, but Oz could not hear what they were saying.

Maggie saw them too. She sighed deeply and turned back to him. 'Don't be sorry, Oz,' she replied. 'No one understands better than me that you can't choose your parents.'

Maggie waved at the figures of Cynthia and Ida who were dancing around near the top of the cliffs and shouted, 'All right! We're coming!'

28

HELLO, GOODBYE

They'd held a sort of council of war: Ulrich laid out on the sofa because he was still weak, his huge feet lolling over the arm; Jean and her on kitchen chairs; and Hoagy keeping order from the old armchair, his eye a disapproving slit.

Jean had been bursting with useless ideas, Hoagy had worn a scowl for the ages, and she had fussed around a bit with tea and drinks, but in the end they had all just listened to what the owl-man had to say. Because he was the only one who could actually help them . . . and it did seem as if he wanted to help them now.

'The best strategy is to make for a part of my world called the Magic Mountains. It's a range of ancient volcanic mountains where the Great O had her sanctuary. The Fathers are thought to be building a fortress of gold there to protect themselves.'

'But how would a gold—?' Jean began. But Hoagy hissed

at her so fiercely that she actually stopped talking. One up for the cat.

For her part, Esme kept her counsel and sipped her brandy. It all felt very surreal to her, like watching a film. She had to keep reminding her brain that what this huge man was saying was not only true, but that she and Hoagy would have to visit the godforsaken places he was describing. You never could tell what would happen next in life, no, you never could tell.

'Of course, I could cross all of us through the portal where you found me, in the woods. But that would be a mistake. There are many who want Maggie Blue, but Maggie Blue will no doubt be in the Magic Mountains, or at least in the vicinity, before too long. Either in accordance with or against her will. In which case, we should cross at the portal nearest to the Magic Mountains.'

'There's more than one?' Jean asked.

His huge yellow owl eyes stared at her. 'There are several. It will perhaps be riskier to cross there but it cannot be helped. Besides,' and here his eyes flicked away from the girl and looked out into the dark garden, 'I don't believe any places of crossing are safe in these times.'

His gaze came back into the room and he first silently interrogated Esme and then turned to Hoagy. 'And the cat must come?' he asked.

The cacophony of wild and angry mewling and fabric clawing that ensued upon this question left no one in doubt as to Hoagy's answer. The owl-man nodded grimly. Clearly he didn't fancy taking her and an ancient cat into a danger zone. Esme couldn't say she blamed him, but there it was – there was no one else.

Ulrich coughed. 'Very well. Moving on.' His huge hands gripped together. 'We need to find a way to get to the other portal in your world. I believe the place we need to reach is called . . .' he hesitated, searching for the right word, 'Wales?'

Esme couldn't help but laugh and Jean's hand shot up in the air as if she was in class. 'I've been there. I went camping—'

The cat hissed at her again, even more violently, and once again she was silenced. The old feline was really coming into his own, Esme noted.

Ulrich was staring at her again. Those eyes were starting to freak her right out. 'How could we reach this place?' he asked her.

Esme only had one idea. She phoned up her friend, Mr Barry – he'd wanted to marry her at one point – and asked to borrow his Volvo. And for some unknown reason, he agreed. Jean clapped her hands in excitement, but everyone else looked pretty grim.

'You need to understand,' Ulrich went on, 'the situation on the Island is volatile. There is war, and there is a lot of danger in trying to rescue this girl. Too many people want her.'

'No one wants her more than us,' Esme said more stoutly than she felt.

The owl-man shook his head. 'That remains to be seen. The girl is very brave, I know that much. But if you come with me, I cannot guarantee anyone's safety, including hers. Do you understand?'

Esme and Hoagy looked at each other for a moment. 'We understand.' Then she examined him more closely. 'And why are you doing this, Ulrich? Why did you decide to help us?'

He shrugged. 'Our chances of finding Maggie Blue, getting her from whomsoever she is with and returning her back here without incident are very, very slight.' He looked at them again. 'You saved my life and I serve you now.' He hesitated then added, his voice waivering a little, 'And I see you are determined. Your love for the girl is very strong.'

Abruptly he got up and strode to the door. 'We should leave as soon as possible.' He wrenched it open and stepped outside, shifting as he did, and in seconds the great owl was flying high into the air.

Jean rushed out to watch him go. 'Wow! I'll never get over that crazy body swap thing he does.' She turned back to them, her eyes blazing with excitement. 'It's *so* cool!'

After the girl had left, with a heavy purring and a nod of approval from the one-eyed cat, Esme and Hoagy decided that there was no way that Jean was coming with them. She was too young and far too enthusiastic. Besides, if something happened to her . . . She was just a girl after all.

So Esme phoned her and told her to meet them at Milton Lodge at nine p.m. the next night. Actually they would be leaving at two p.m. Esme felt bad about this deceit, but it was for the best, and frankly the drive to Wales would be hairy enough: she hadn't been behind the wheel of any vehicle since around 1997. Not that she'd mentioned it to Mr Barry; the information was on a strictly need-to-know basis – even Hoagy was in the dark on this one.

They spent the next morning getting everything packed and ready, and she had instructed Ulrich, who by this time had returned from his impromptu flight, and Hoagy to lie low until she returned. Because before she vanished on this mad-cap adventure, she needed to do one thing, something she had been avoiding for years now.

Anything might happen there and it would, without doubt, be dangerous for them. But, on balance, it was better than sitting around doing nothing, getting drunk and feeling like hell. She knew Maggie would do the same for her; she could not let her down. But just at that moment, she had other things on her mind.

After the packing, Esme had done her hair into such a pristine beehive that Hoagy had nearly passed out from the hairspray fumes. She'd made sure her glasses were well polished, her shoes clean and her uniform of navy-blue skirt and white blouse nicely pressed. She had not had a drink since the day before yesterday, and she had brushed her teeth. So far, so good.

But her palms were sticky as she walked up the spotless front path through the perfect and dull little garden and rang the smart brushed-chrome bell. There was an endless wait in the boiling sun until the door finally swung open and there, in the doorway, looking forbidding in a floor-length black dress with stately shoulder pads, stood Ms Muriel McCrab. (Did she ever dress casually? Esme wondered.)

As the headmistress's cold eyes took in the unexpected presence of Esme Durand on her doorstep, yet again, the latter concurrently realised that her power of speech had momentarily deserted her. After standing for some time, spluttering like a goldfish that'd been scooped out of its bowl, Esme managed to say in a hoarse whisper, 'I need to talk to you.'

Ms McCrab edged back, almost imperceptibly, to allow her visitor the chance to enter her dark house. But Esme didn't pick up on this subtle body movement. Instead, once the first rambling words were out, it seemed that she couldn't stop.

'Of course, I'm a much weaker person than you,' Esme began. 'You know, very emotional and everything, although I've tried to work on that. Not on emotion, that's good, but on, you know, self-compassion and everything . . . not that that's going too well.' She broke off into a nervous giggle.

Ms McCrab raised one hand a little, as if in self-defence. Her mouth had opened into a small circle and she seemed to be on the verge of making some kind of noise, but she had no chance. She glanced surreptitiously over at her neighbours' houses on either side, but thankfully no one seemed to be around.

'I never actually said anything, but I was quite devastated, you know, when you wouldn't see me any more. Actually, I was heartbroken, that's what I was. And I still am. I got better, I got over it, you know, day by day, with some help, but . . . well, the nub of it is, the *thing* is . . .'

Here Esme took a disturbingly deep breath. 'The thing is . . . well, but I am going away today, and the reality is that I may not come back. And I still care about you. I wanted to say it before I disappear for ever, which is more than likely, if I'm not actually going mad here, which also seems quite possible.'

Ms McCrab's face had now assumed a rigid shocked expression; her eyelids blinked up and down a lot. Finally she spoke.

'What are you talking about? You need to calm down.' She glanced around again and whispered, 'Why don't you come inside?'

But Esme didn't respond to this. She had paused to wipe the sweat from her brow; she had calmed down a little.

'You're the only person who knows where I'm going, or even that I'm going away. I hope to see you again, of course. But I just wanted to say all the things I never did, just in case, and to say, er, well, to say goodbye.'

'Esme!' Ms McCrab's face was exasperated. 'I don't know what you're talking about and I don't know where you're going. What *is* going on?'

Esme laughed suddenly. She'd planned to be so clear, but it had all come out in a rush and evidently she hadn't made any sense whatsoever. She took another deep breath. 'I'm going to look for Maggie . . . in this other world, if it really exists. You know, the one your father went to.'

There was a long silence. Finally Ms McCrab spoke. 'You really believe she's there?'

Esme nodded. 'I can't abandon her. And anyway, she means too much to me now.'

The headmistress's face was rigid. 'I see. Well, take care of yourself. I'm glad you've told me. And I hope to see you again.'

And she shut the door, just like that.

Esme stood on the front doorstep in shock. There wasn't any more to say, but it had been so abrupt. She wanted to ring the bell again, but why? It had already been a fairly excruciating experience. She stood there for a minute or so, then slowly walked back down the path and out of sight.

On the other side of the door, Ms McCrab had crumpled into a heap on the hall floor. She had been holding her breath, holding herself together, a tight knot in her throat, but when she heard Esme finally walking away, she burst into floods of tears.

29

THE TERRIBLE ONES

The white crow landed on her shoulder as she and Oz walked round the edge of the lake and began climbing the slippery pink rock once again. Maggie felt afraid now . . . her moment of transcendence and understanding had faded in the white-time light; things didn't seem so clear any more.

The knife was in her pocket and she still wore the moon witch's cloak – she felt safer in it somehow. She pictured the moon witch writhing and gasping on the ground, blood pouring out of its side where she had stabbed it. Then the white transparent ball rolling away, like woodlice do when you touch them. Even though its intention had been to kill her, she hoped it was not dead . . .

'Maggie?'

She realised Oz was talking to her and she saw fear in his eyes. She tuned into the voices just above her. Cynthia's agitated face leant over the cliff edge and Maggie could hear what she was saying now.

'There's some horrible things coming towards us, fast! Enormous snakes!'

They exchanged a glance and then scrambled up to the cave as fast as they could. Maggie could see two writhing black bodies moving through the trees at great speed, and they were heading straight for the pink cliffs.

Beside her, Oz said in a small voice, 'The Terrible Ones.'

'Are you sure?'

'Yes. I can hear them in the air already. Can't you?'

Maggie stood still and realised there was a very faint low humming that seemed to be coming from her own head. 'That's them?'

The boy nodded.

'What are those awful things?' Cynthia asked.

Maggie noticed with counter-productive satisfaction that her mum sounded afraid now, that she had lost her annoying Zen glow.

Oz explained as briefly as he could, putting emphasis on the fact that these creatures were coming for Maggie and were impossible to destroy.

Cynthia listened closely then began pacing up and down the little plateau outside the cave. 'Where on earth is Roda? He should be back by now. He could take Maggie on his back. Oh, where is he?'

'Maybe he's abandoned you again,' Maggie said maliciously. But her mum didn't seem to notice her tone. She started pacing again, still muttering to herself.

'Abandoned me? Yes, maybe he has. Couldn't quite bear to let me die a horrible death, but then thought he'd leave me to it. That's very possible, yes. Or maybe he's dead.' She stopped in her tracks and stared at them all intently. 'We have to act.' She looked back out towards the forest. 'We don't have much time.'

'What are you doing?' Maggie asked, freaked out again by her mum's change in character: she had never ever been like this before. She used to be unable to choose between different brands of pasta in the supermarket; she would run out crying instead of making a decision . . .

And now Cynthia Brown was already heaving herself up to the top of the cliff. Standing a few feet above them, she said, 'You forget – I know this place well. I used to come here all the time when I was young . . . with Roda. And there's somewhere we can hide. Come on.'

The three children looked at each other blankly, but as no other suggestions were forthcoming, they followed Cynthia up the cliff and then the mountainside beyond as fast as they could.

'Come on!' Cynthia called back. 'Hurry!'

But it was heavy going. The grass thinned almost immediately, making way for an uneven red rocky terrain full of ruts and pools of mud. Oz eagerly scurried after her mum, but Ida fell behind and barely seemed able to put one foot in front of the other. So Maggie grabbed her hand and pulled her along, even though her own legs were already aching. As she did so, she marvelled at her reed-thin mother, skipping up the mountainside like a deer in her weird cultish robe.

Beyond the top of the brown-red mountain, they could see the grander purple peaks of the Magic Mountains in the distance. The white crow was flying right above Maggie and she could feel their connection, the thin tremulous thread vibrating between them. She felt its fear too . . . she understood implicitly that the Great O would not be able to help them much in the face of the Terrible Ones . . . she was not strong enough . . . not yet.

Maggie stopped for a moment and looked down into the valley. Ida stopped beside her, breathless. She did not seem to be focusing on anything; her eyes were expressionless.

'Ida . . . Are you OK?'

No reply, so Maggie squeezed her hand and after a long moment the returning squeeze came back, but Ida still didn't speak or show any emotion. It seemed like this was the only way she could deal with what was happening, so Maggie just kept pulling her up the steep slope.

The events of the last few hours swirled around in Maggie's head as they climbed – her mum's curious transformation into a not-completely-useless person, the revelation that Roda was her father, and the understanding that came with it – that she was a half-shifter and from another world. In some strange way, this information eased Maggie's mind. She wasn't just 'weird' in a run-of-the-mill, loser, suburban way that her bullies had always thought; she was from another world, she *was* special. It was why she could cross, why she could hear Hoagy speak and why Dot had been so excited about her. And it also explained why Lion had never loved her . . . she'd always felt that.

But it still didn't explain why the Great O needed her . . . OK, she was special, different, but so what? She knew the Great O was still weak; that she needed to get back to the Magic Mountains to regain her strength. So why not just go back? Why not leave her and fly there right now? It didn't make sense.

Maggie remembered asking Dot why the Great O didn't just destroy whomsoever she wanted, and the little moon witch had got annoyed with her . . . what was it she had said? Something about the Great O being subject to those on earth . . . that she wasn't separate . . . that she needed them too . . . Maggie couldn't quite remember and there was no time now . . .

The wind started to pick up as they gained altitude and the red grit flew into their eyes and mouths. It was getting warmer too. Maggie was sweating in the thick moon-witch cloak and it wasn't long before they had to stop again. They all rested for a moment and drank the last of Oz's water. They weren't too far now from the very top.

Maggie examined her mum again: her white robe, her skin and her hair were all covered in red dust, but her eyes were sparkling with excitement. She was high on the danger.

'Why are we doing this?' Maggie asked abruptly. 'There's nowhere to hide up here: they'll just pick us off.'

But her mum was unerringly, irritatingly confident. 'There's a caldera at the top of this mountain; it was formed by a huge volcanic eruption here thousands of years ago. There's a beautiful blue pool there now, but it's full of acid, the water is deadly.' She looked at Oz. 'Even if it is impossible to destroy these snake things, as you say, I think a dip in there should at least slow them down for a bit.'

'But how are we going to get them in there? Jump in first?' Maggie demanded.

Cynthia smiled maddeningly at her. 'I've told you, Maggie, I know this place very well.'

Suddenly the white crow wheeled above them, screeching violently. Maggie looked down the mountainside and saw with horror that the two enormous black serpents had already reached the lake. They paused there for a moment – it was almost as if they were sniffing the ground like dogs – and then suddenly they began to climb up towards them.

The humming was getting louder and it droned uncomfortably in Maggie's head, blocking out other thoughts. Feelings of dread flooded through her and made her want to stop moving altogether, to just sit down and give up. Perhaps it would be better just to accept her fate?

She watched her mum dispassionately . . . she seemed to be dancing up and down on the spot, screaming and shouting. But Maggie could barely make out what she was saying. Then Cynthia lunged at her, her hands grabbing at her body. She realised her mum was trying to get the bloodied black cloak off her. Maggie began to scream and fight back, until finally Cynthia wrenched the filthy garment away.

Panting from the struggle, Cynthia turned to Oz and Ida and screamed, 'I need one of you!'

She was screaming against the humming noise that now pounded in all their heads. Ida remained completely passive and didn't look up, but Oz, sweet Oz, stepped forward at once.

'I'll help,' he said.

Without further explanation, Cynthia put the cloak over his head. It completely swamped him so that he looked like a bizarre little gnome.

Her mum took his hand. 'Be brave, Oz,' she shouted. 'I promise I know what I'm doing. Nothing's going to happen to you. But you must be brave.' She looked over at Maggie and Ida. 'You two, go and hide! Quickly! Don't let them see Maggie.'

'But Mum!' Maggie screamed.

'There's no time. Just go!'

The humming in her head was unbearable now and Maggie's eyesight was blurring slightly. The figure of her mum swayed and fizzled in front of her.

'GO!' it screamed.

Maggie saw Oz's face turn to her – it was pale with fear. She reached her hand out to him, but her mum was already dragging him away.

At that moment the white crow slipped into her pocket. Maggie grabbed Ida's hand and, seeing a small outcrop of red dusty rocks a little way above them, she dragged her over there and they hunkered down out of sight.

Maggie peered around the stones and watched as Cynthia hauled little Oz towards the top. Beside her, Ida was leaning against a rock and staring into space. She hadn't spoken for hours but now she remarked, shouting against the humming, 'She wants them to think it's you.'

Maggie spun round to look at her in astonishment. 'What?'

'I said, your mum wants the snakes to think Oz is you . . . that's why she put the cloak on him.'

'Do you think Oz is going to be OK?'

Ida shrugged. 'She sounded pretty sure about the whole thing. But . . .'

Maggie never found out what Ida's further concerns about her mother's plan were, because at that moment the humming vibrated so violently through her body that her brain was too full of the dull roaring sound to do anything else but survive it.

She flattened herself onto the ground and red dust filled her eyes and her throat. But she just managed to see, silhouetted against the sky, two figures standing at what must be the edge of the volcano, its rim. Her heart was in her mouth – why had she let Oz go? He was so little, and maybe her mum was crazy.

The thick sinuous bodies sped past them. When the beasts were almost upon them, the two figures of Oz and her mum jumped and disappeared into the caldera. The first snake careered over the edge after them. A few seconds later, a faint smell of burning reached them and a hideous agonised screaming that Maggie thought might rip her mind apart.

Maggie found herself on her feet screaming, 'Mum!' Ida dragged her back down, but it was too late. The second serpent hesitated just at the edge and then slowly it turned its great head towards them.

Maggie and Ida hugged each other tightly, huddling behind the stones, both of them shaking with terror. The awful screaming kept on and their bodies vibrated against each other, filled with the unearthly drone. Then suddenly a pair of hideous white eyes and a black mouth, wide open, filled with little sharp white teeth, reared up at them over the red rocks. Maggie screamed and pushed Ida away from her as the smooth leathery body fell towards her. But Ida still held tightly onto her hand. Maggie fought as best she could, but the thing wrapped itself around her legs and chest and pulled at her with brute strength. Her hand was finally wrenched from Ida's and she heard her friend scream.

All the breath left her body and for a moment – time

stopped. Then there was only the noise shaking inside her and the squeezing at her chest. She tried to look back, but she realised she was already moving at speed back down the volcano's side, back the way she had come.

She managed to breathe in a huge gasp of air and understood that she was being held in the tail of the beast as it slid back down the mountainside at speed. Its skin was cold and smooth. She could feel the white crow writhing and wriggling in her pocket, trying to get out as she was dragged roughly over the ground. Her knees were in agony and bleeding freely. She managed to turn round. But the beast gripped her more tightly and she was stuck.

Flashing suddenly through the sky, she saw Roda high above, screeching wildly and flying at speed towards the volcano's peak. Following him were several smaller birds, like little swallows but with bright turquoise feathers. Maggie thought she could still hear Ida screaming way behind her, and the excruciating cries of the other beast.

The pain of her skin being ripped from her legs was so excruciating she too started howling and crying. Through her tears she saw the tiny bright birds again, flying swiftly, following her and the beast, though Roda was no longer with them. But she had no time to wonder where he was, because as the snake lurched back down over the pink cliffs, careering towards the lake at high speed, her head connected with a slab of the rose-pink rock, and everything went black.

30

ROAD TRIPPERS

Hoagy had been dozing heavily on the old couch ever since Esme had announced a mystery errand, which was so obviously another visit to see Ms McCrab it was embarrassing. But now he started violently awake and his heart was pounding. He looked around the deserted room, dust motes caught in the thick sunlight, there was nothing there.

Perhaps it was just a bad dream, although they'd mostly cleared up since he'd stopped nibbling on that box of stale After Eights he'd found under the piano. His whiskers twitched – what had he been dreaming about? It was something . . . someone . . . he closed his eye and tried to return to it. Almost at once, his eye popped open again – Maggie, something was wrong with Maggie.

Despite his run-ins over the years with suburban witches, the wild forest men of Barnet, the shamans of Finchley Central and most recently, of course, another world, Hoagy was still a cynic who always looked for a rational explanation: too much chlorine in the water supply in the case of the Barnet forest dwellers. But this was different. His whole body, his scruffy fur and his abundant whiskers vibrated with it – he *felt* it. Maggie was in trouble, no, worse than that, danger . . . mortal danger.

He leapt down from the sofa and rushed out of the back door and round the house. The owl-man was just finishing packing up the old Volvo and to the cat's surprise, he saw the girl Jean jamming her own small rucksack into the back of the car. She turned and smiled at him smugly.

Oh Lord, Hoagy thought.

Ignoring her, he rushed up to Ulrich and started scratching at his great ankles. 'Maggie is in danger. I can feel it.'

The man's huge eyes honed in on him and he nodded. 'I feel it too. We must get to the portal as quickly as we can. It's our best hope.'

The old cat felt his heart had turned to lead – if only he could have stopped Maggie being taken that fateful night, if only he could have helped his beloved friend.

Jean had perched herself on the rusty car bonnet and her leg was incessantly bouncing up and down again. Hoagy ran up to her and started hissing violently until she finally got the message and got into the car. Ulrich followed suit. They weren't going to waste a minute. They had to get on the road and get to Maggie Blue as fast as they could.

When Esme got back to her flat, she found Ulrich, Hoagy and Jean all crammed into the car outside waiting for her with everything packed. For a moment, her head still spinning from her disastrous and embarrassing monologue on Muriel's front doorstep, the sight of the huge man, fat cat and over-excited girl all crammed into a yellow '90s Volvo made her want to both laugh and cry, or more likely have a hysterical breakdown. However, the five eyes staring expectantly back at her were deadly serious.

Esme pulled herself together, strode forwards and yanked open the back door where Jean was sitting determinedly beside Hoagy. 'There is no way you're coming, Jean. I cannot allow it.' The girl made no sign of moving. 'I'd pretty much be abducting you as far as your parents are concerned. I mean, I could be sent to jail or something.'

But Jean only smiled at her maddeningly.

'Get out of the car *now*.' Esme tried to inject some authority into her voice.

'It's all cool,' Jean said. 'Ulrich sorted it.'

Her arrogant manner annoyed Esme. 'How could he *sort* it?'

Jean laughed with delight. 'Turns out he can control people's minds, like, really easily. I wish I could do that.'

Esme looked at the motionless mound of man currently bursting out of the front seat. And her eyes were drawn once again to his enormous gnarled hands. They were immensely powerful – they looked full of violence. And she was also to understand he could control people's minds? She did not like it at all. She felt afraid of him suddenly.

Accordingly, the man seemed to read her thoughts. He turned to her. 'I won't harm you,' he said. 'Believe that. I may have lost my path, but I am a noble warrior and you may be thankful for that one day.'

Having said his piece, he turned back and sat motionless, staring at the drive once again.

'What is going on?' Esme demanded.

Jean giggled maddeningly again. 'He came round to my house and he told my mum I was going to a young socialists' summer camp in Wales – I told him what to say, obviously – and she just nodded and said wonderful. And then I told him to ask her for £200 and she just got up on a chair and got it out of this tin on top of the kitchen cupboards, pushed right to the back, that I've never even noticed before. And she just gave it to me! Ha! It was hilarious.'

Esme shook her head. 'I don't know what you told your mother and I don't care. You can't go, Jean – it's impossible. Do you realise this is dangerous? Or else mad? Or both? We may not come back. Hoagy and I may not come back. Do you understand that?'

The cat made a purring noise at that moment that only Ulrich could understand as 'Speak for yourself, love.' But the owl-man felt no immediate need to translate.

'You can't risk it,' Esme continued. 'Or else nothing at

all will happen. It will be a wild goose chase. But we're both old. It doesn't matter about us.'

This time the old cat looked at her and hissed. Esme rolled her eyes at him. 'Come on, Hoagy, it's kind of true.'

Another deep purring sound was emitted. Again, Ulrich didn't bother to translate. Insults were not helpful at this point, if they ever were.

'Don't you need someone who isn't old and knackered to help out?' Jean said cheekily. Esme could see the girl was buzzing with it all. 'No offence, of course.'

'It's not about that, dearie. Don't you see? We might not come back. Do you understand? We really might die.'

Esme realised as she spoke that she'd barely acknowledged it herself. She had no idea what she was doing. She felt like a wet lettuce suddenly . . . limp and without energy. She was lost.

And she was shocked by the steely look that came into Jean's eyes – and anger too. 'You're not taking this away from me. I've been waiting my whole life for something like this. If you don't take me with you, I'll call the police. I'll tell them Maggie is missing and that a strange man has abducted you. I'll give them the car plates and everything. You'll never make it.'

Esme was astonished. 'You'd stop us from helping Maggie?'

'And how are you going to help her exactly?'

'I don't exactly know. But would you do that?'

Jean nodded vigorously. 'Yes. It's my fate. I have to come with you. I won't let you go without me.'

The owl-man turned his head round again and said in a flat voice, 'She is extremely determined. I don't sense anything will deter her. And she is serious in her threat.' Then his meaty head rotated back again.

It moved like an owl's, Esme noted with an accompanying sense of revulsion.

She shook her head. 'Fine. But if you die, it's not my fault.'

'Fine,' the girl repeated stubbornly from the back.

All resistance left her. She no longer cared, she just wanted to get going and help Maggie. Everything else was a stupid waste of time.

Jean, seeing that she'd won, clapped her long hands together. 'Come on! Let's go!' she cried excitedly.

Esme frowned. 'Well, wait a minute, dearie. I have to go in and have a pee and change my shoes. I can't drive in these.' And she lifted up one of her black Mary Janes. She had an old pair of trainers that she was planning to wear for the purpose, shoes she had never previously left the house in.

The old cat was seen to half-shut his eye and begin a deep, very loud purr that Esme suspected was sarcastic. Well, whatever, she needed to pee. Not everyone could do it on the lawn.

When she came out again they were all still there, much

as if they hadn't moved or spoken. She threw a few more things into the back of the car and got into the driver's seat. After much messing about with the chair height and position, she finally turned the key and tried to remember about clutch control. It stalled... she tried again... it stalled. There was complete silence around her, as if everyone in the car was holding their breath. She pressed her mouth firmly together and tried again. This time the ancient car spluttered into life and lurched out of the driveway into the oncoming traffic. Hoagy hissed and even the owl-man looked somewhat perturbed. Only Jean remained excited.

As Esme manoeuvred the yellow Volvo onto the road and managed to get it into second without too much trouble, Jean wound down the window and shouted to the waiting traffic, 'We're going to rescue Maggie Blue!'

And as the car merged into the afternoon traffic, Esme sincerely hoped that this was true.

THE END

ACKNOWLEDGEMENTS

Thank you to the wonderful Bella Pearson; Sandra Dieckmann for a cover that is even more beautiful than the first; Hannah Featherstone; Nick, Juno and Winnie (my constant writing companion); and my friends Cress and Ana who, in their different ways, helped me through the darkest time in my life – I wouldn't have made it without you.

'After such a *"lovely evening…"'* Cesare's amusement was deeper now, his accented English doing even more to make her breathless '…there is only one way to end it, no?'

For an instant he held Carla's gaze in the dim light, daring her to accept, to concede, to do what he wanted her to do—what he'd wanted from the first moment he'd set eyes on her.

'Like this,' he said.

He stretched his hand out, long fingers tilting up her face to his as his mouth lowered to hers. Slowly, sensuously, savouring. With skill, with expertise, with a lifetime of experience in how to let his lips glide over hers, to let his mouth open hers to his, to taste the sweetness within. As soft, as sensual as silk velvet.

She drowned in it. A thousand nerve-endings fired as he made free with her mouth, his long fingers still holding her. And when he had done he released her, drew back his hand, let it curve around the driving wheel.

He smiled. *'Buone notte,'* he said softly.

From Mistress to Wife

From the bedroom—to the altar!

Eloise and Carla have never expected irresistible
passion—until they meet the powerful alpha
billionaires who will steal their innocence. But nights
of passion can have unexpected consequences…

When Eloise Dean falls at Vito Viscari's feet,
they are both overcome with a desire
they can neither resist nor deny!

Claiming His Scandalous Love-Child

Carla Charteris knows falling for the enigmatic
Count of Mantegna will only bring heartache, but
what will happen when temptation proves irresistible?

Carrying His Scandalous Heir

Available now!

You won't want to miss this passionately sexy duet
from Julia James!

as if they hadn't moved or spoken. She threw a few more things into the back of the car and got into the driver's seat. After much messing about with the chair height and position, she finally turned the key and tried to remember about clutch control. It stalled . . . she tried again . . . it stalled. There was complete silence around her, as if everyone in the car was holding their breath. She pressed her mouth firmly together and tried again. This time the ancient car spluttered into life and lurched out of the driveway into the oncoming traffic. Hoagy hissed and even the owl-man looked somewhat perturbed. Only Jean remained excited.

As Esme manoeuvred the yellow Volvo onto the road and managed to get it into second without too much trouble, Jean wound down the window and shouted to the waiting traffic, 'We're going to rescue Maggie Blue!'

And as the car merged into the afternoon traffic, Esme sincerely hoped that this was true.

THE END

ACKNOWLEDGEMENTS

Thank you to the wonderful Bella Pearson; Sandra Dieckmann for a cover that is even more beautiful than the first; Hannah Featherstone; Nick, Juno and Winnie (my constant writing companion); and my friends Cress and Ana who, in their different ways, helped me through the darkest time in my life – I wouldn't have made it without you.